Mutable Passions

CHARLOTTE BRONTË:
A DISQUIETING AFFAIR

PHILIP DENT

Matador
9 Priory Business Park,
Wistow Road, Kibworth Beauchamp,
Leicestershire. LE8 0RX
Tel: (+44) 116 279 2299
Fax: (+44) 116 279 2277
Email: books@troubador.co.uk
Web: www.troubador.co.uk/matador

ISBN 978 1785890 932

British Library Cataloguing in Publication Data.
A catalogue record for this book is available from the British Library.

Printed and bound in the UK by TJ International, Padstow, Cornwall
Typeset in 10.5pt Palatino by Troubador Publishing Ltd, Leicester, UK

Matador is an imprint of Troubador Publishing Ltd

*To my mother who, in her ninety-fifth year,
finds sufficient value still to prolong the struggle
for another day.*

Chapter One

Charlotte Brontë lived with her father at the parsonage in Haworth. Her five siblings were all dead: Emily and Anne following their brother Branwell to their graves a few years earlier. Her older sisters, Maria and Elizabeth, perished in infancy and her mother died when Charlotte was a child.

Dreams of past pleasures were all she had left to cling to, but life for Charlotte was removed from the dream-like imaginings allied with restful sleep. Memories were tainted with sadness and dreams all crushed beneath the might of nightmares. Rooms that were once warmed with gaiety and poetry trembled, troubled by the cold-hearted dance of death's empty husks.

Nausea and headaches blighted her days, and disease and illness were never far away, lurking ominously in the bracken, in the trees and in murky streams. Impatient to strike, sometimes cruelly when, after a protracted period of suffering, a light had begun to lighten life's burdens.

Loneliness was the worst.

Reverend Patrick Brontë, Charlotte's ageing father, was an eccentric white-haired man. Prone to bronchial infection, he wrapped copious layers of white linen around his neck to ward away illness. The layers increased with the advancing years, stiffening the already stern cleric.

Tetchy with old age and with a disintegrating body that had grown dismissive of the commands that in youth were instantaneous, Mr Brontë was able to provide little by way of cheerful society, and smooth life's fractious journey for his last surviving daughter. Nor could he replenish the kindred spirit that Charlotte craved most: genial company that might help stem the tremors, erupting with heart-wrenching regularity from the pit of loneliness.

On good days Charlotte wrote for hours. Other days she could not write at all and her thoughts drifted, yielding to unsettling visitations. Haunting spectres that circled in daylight and in darkness; images of deceased siblings that, with sickness and headaches, obliterated the spark of literary creation. Days, sometimes weeks passed when little by way of progress was achieved with her novel, *Villette*. The wasted days rankled, fuelling her frustration and deepening her despair.

Charlotte ached most for amiable company, for the companionship of like-minded friends, or for some other consuming activity apart from writing. Something that might complement the solitary life necessary for an author, for an author deprived of the sisterhood that had helped hone her writing and had steered her toward success. Friendship of the kind she had known and lived with since childhood: a substitute for sisters lost to the eternal night. She was desperate for something or someone that might help smother the bitter assault of memory. Memories evoked only heartache and sorrow, revisiting repeatedly the tortuous paths of Emily and Anne's last flights: their determination to breathe another heart-wrought, consumptive breath in order that they might live another day, another hour. Images of Branwell, his drunken rages and the self-inflicted wounds, which, with illness, would consume him. The less precise recollections of Maria and Elizabeth, sisters long since dead. Memories that broke her heart again and again.

Snowfall signalled the start of another winter, dreary days and interminable cold nights when Charlotte might be prisoner to the weather for weeks. It was in the gloom of those dark winter months when inconvenienced by snow, when the steep roads around Haworth were rendered impassable by uncompromising deep drifts that Charlotte's headaches worsened. Sickness obliterated an already scant appetite, denying her the nourishment and nutrients necessary for a productive mind. But worse, unable to visit Ellen Nussey, long-time friend and the one person capable of lifting Charlotte's spirits from the consuming dark void, and for her to visit Charlotte, her depression deepened.

Winter was always the worst time of the year. It was the loneliest time, more so since Emily, Anne and Branwell had surrendered to the lure of eternal rest and were tucked secure in their graves, untroubled by the ills that torment living flesh. Writing was no longer the fulfilling and engaging occupation that it once was, its pleasures being lost or diminished. Gone was the confident song of Emily's strong voice and her strident demands to forsake inhibiting feminine sensitivities and apply greater malice to characters rendered already brutal. Flown too, soon after, Anne, and the calm, reflective manner in which she pleaded for the opposing qualities demanded of her sister: for a softening of the unsettling characteristics apportioned to Bertha Mason in *Jane Eyre*.

Night after night, Charlotte sat alone, ponderous and fretful, sometimes tearful. Her father was in his seventies and would not live forever. With his passing another parson would be employed in his place, and the parsonage would no longer be her home. Soon Charlotte would be truly alone: alone and homeless.

Chapter Two

Sitting one evening in the dining room beside an insipid fire, Charlotte was irritable, tugging, for the umpteenth time, the thick beige shawl she wore tighter about her shoulders. Glancing intermittently, and with undisguised ire, to the servant, Tabitha Aykroyd – known affectionately as Tabby – noisily clearing the crockery and cutlery. Every attempt to write was interrupted by a dropped fork, by the clash of dishes and pots, or a groan from the servant's wet lips as she limped about the room, rubbing a troublesome thigh (the legacy of an injury sustained some years earlier after slipping on ice one winter).

Once her concentration was lost completely, Charlotte sighed; she removed her spectacles and set her work aside. Nipping her lips tight together, she stood and picked up the poker from the hearth and stoked the dying grey embers in the grate. Afterwards, she stood with her back to the still dismal fire and observed the servant going about her work. Charlotte smiled, and her lips moved but it was Tabby that spoke first.

'It's times as these you'll most miss your sisters...' Seeing the abrupt change wash over Charlotte's features, the servant fell silent, but she smiled and then continued, 'a good man will warm you better that a few dying cinders.'

'You are perhaps right, Tabby,' Charlotte said, a shallow smile forming and lifting the gloom from melancholic looks, 'but good men about Haworth are few. And in any case I'm gone thirty-five; a good man's eyes would flash past me were there younger, prettier girls about.'

'You're a famous writer, Charlotte!' Tabby reminded her, as she hobbled toward the door. She turned sharply back. 'You've men from Manchester to London calling on you,' she said, shaking her head and continuing in a voice that climbed an octave higher, 'yet you turn your head from the men in the parish.'

'From whom have I—!'

'The farmers, mill workers—'

'I do not, Tabby. You imagine it.'

'The farmers and mill workers, I suppose, are not a good enough match now you're a famous author?'

Charlotte's eyes widened with indignation. 'One man, should he take my fancy, is as good as the next, be he a farm labourer living on the moors about Haworth or a lawyer from London,' she said. Her irritation softened and she giggled. 'Provided his ears and nose are of reasonable proportion, and he doesn't smell like the sheep on the moors.'

'There you go, mocking—'

'Seriously, Tabby, I mock no one, but honestly, who—'

'What then of your father's curate? His roving eye—'

'Mr Nicholls!' Charlotte interrupted, mildly outraged. 'I could no more kiss the lips of a man with a beard as big as rooks' nests than I could yours, Tabby,' she said and then laughed.

'Aye, and that'd give the gossipy village folk sour fodder to chew on!' Tabby said, chuckling and shaking her head. She hobbled from the dining room, laughing all the way back to the kitchen.

Charlotte returned her attention to the fire. Raking thoroughly the spent ash, and then standing once again with her back to the heat. Staring abstractedly at the pencil sketches of her sisters, Emily and Anne, set in frames and arranged on a cabinet. Heartstrings tightened and tears flooded her eyes; the affectionate tug of sibling love was as real and vivid as when they were alive and in the room with her. Charlotte's thoughts drifted, effortlessly conjuring memories of happier times when, with Emily and Anne and Branwell, they ran free on the moors on idyllic summer days, wrote poetry and prose in the studious silence of cold winter evenings.

Charlotte picked up the pictures of her sisters and kissed each image in turn and then set them back down on the cabinet. Returning the sketches to their former position with tender precision.

It seemed like only hours since Emily and Anne were in the room with her. Discussing, analysing and fiercely arguing the merits of each other's writing; in her heart they were there still, Branwell also, alive and real, even though they were gone, flown away like last night's dream. The richness of those exhilarating days could not come again.

Blinking away tears, Charlotte turned and walked disconsolately toward the door, taking the lighted candle from the dining room table. After opening the door she shuffled back round, glimpsed the images one last time and whispered goodnight; and then stepped into the draughty hall. She closed the door softly behind her, tearful and trembling; the pain of parting stung like it always had.

The sound of the servant, working later than usual in the kitchen, returned a smile to Charlotte's tremulous lips.

'The fire's not out yet, Tabby,' she called to her.

'It'll have gone out before I'm done,' the servant called back, amid the scuffing of footsteps and the clatter of crockery, 'but fret not, Charlotte, not a spark will remain or I'll empty my bladder on it.'

Charlotte shook her head and her smile widened.

'Goodnight, Tabby.'

'Goodnight, Charlotte… sleep tight.'

Charlotte dragged her weary body up the steep stairs, one step after another. On reaching the top and passing by her father's room, she angled her head and listened; his intermittent snort reassured her that he slept soundly in his bed. She continued to her room, stepped inside and then closed the door on another dreary and predictable day. The night, though, had only just begun.

Sleep, in the fitful interludes that it came, returned life to lost sisters and a brother. Soon she would hear the giddy music of Emily's voice calling out her name; she would see her vibrant spectre charging about the vast moorland with her mastiff, Keeper, bounding along at her side. And Anne's beguiling image would delight no less, with her contrasting gentle manner and the delicate voice of a cherished sister whose captivating violet gaze was rivalled only by that of angels. The images would momentarily enthral her but then the opulence of her dream would be shattered, annihilated by the drunken ranting of a disillusioned and deluded brother, whose tortured soul only the new morning could cure.

Chapter Three

The bitter winter morning began as the day always did. Mr Brontë, attired in his nightgown, after stretching and yawning, heaved up the heavy sash window in his room and, undeterred by the snow driven inside and upon him, thrust his head out into the invigorating freshness. Resting his hands on the windowsill, he stood awhile, purging his lungs in the cold, clean air as he scanned the snow-clad buildings, the shivering trees and the surrounding white moorland. He reached inside, found his pistol and, smiling wryly, pointed the firearm at the church steeple and pulled the trigger. The ricocheting bullet silenced the sparrows chirruping in the bushes, but roused the rooks and set them dancing and squawking in the treetops.

Charlotte's eyes were wide and staring like someone suddenly traumatised but she smiled. The explosive early morning alarm call, though reassuring, startled her still, even though she had listened to its violence at the same hour for as long as she could remember.

'Dear, Papa...' she uttered distractedly, and with fond annoyance. 'I look to the day I am no longer forced to suffer the racket of that thing discharging its bullet of a morning.'

Downstairs, she could hear the servants in the kitchen busy preparing breakfast. She threw back the covers and leaped from her warm bed, into the cold uncertainty of the new morning. After dressing quickly, she braced herself for another day of heartache, of headaches and nausea and then she descended the stairs.

*

Arthur Bell Nicholls, Patrick Bronte's curate, strode briskly if cautiously, over the new-fallen snow, toward the church. Frowning, he looked up to the leaden sky, but turned swiftly from it when the descending cold crystals stung his eyes; and he looked instead to the intricately patterned snowflakes swirling pleasingly about him in the light breeze, watching as they alighted daintily upon his coat.

Upright and serious, Mr Nicholls' true emotions were concealed behind a stoic, religious veil – or his beard. Invariably polite, he acknowledged everyone with the same severe gaze (his lips seeming never quite able to form the smile that he might wish for), a nod and a kindly word, whether they were highbred or lowbred, whether they attended his church or they did not.

He stepped under the vestibule and out of the falling snow, sighing, stamping his feet and loosening his coat collar as he shuffled toward the church door. The door opened suddenly and Charlotte rushed out. Their eyes met briefly, fitfully like irate lovers, midway into a quarrel that neither could expect to win. Mr Nicholls' face illuminated nevertheless, and he smiled and doffed his hat in the gentlemanly manner that came naturally to him.

'Good day, Miss Brontë, I…'

Charlotte, pulling her scarf up over her mouth, nodded muted acknowledgement, flashed an indifferent stare and stepped swiftly by without uttering a single word, a single syllable.

Mr Nicholls, affronted somewhat, stood and watched

9

as Charlotte stepped out into the snow and hurried away. The curate's smile faded a little more with each retreating step, but his wounded eye stalked her until she was lost to distance and to the falling snow. Sighing, he stepped inside the dimly lit church and then closed the door. Distracted and thoughtful, he stumbled into his employer who stood with his head bowed over the stone bearing the inscription,

"Emily Jane Brontë, 1818–1848".

'Mr Brontë, I…' Mr Nicholls uttered, smiling and gesticulating by way of an apology for his clumsiness.

Mr Brontë turned and eyed the curate with indifference for some seconds, before returning his soulless gaze to the tombstone of his daughter. Mr Nicholls, shuffling uneasily, removed his hat and then he, too, adopted the same stance, the same inexpressive stare, and then fixed his gaze upon Emily's tombstone. His thoughts, though, were not with Emily. He appeared nervous and impatient and the instant Mr Bronte's prayers were done, the curate cleared his throat noisily, and then the men's eyes met.

'Charlotte…' Mr Nicholls began, gesticulating uncomfortably. 'I… I passed her on the way to church,' he said, through lips stiffened still from the cold. 'I see her most days of the week and each day she wears the same sad mask of a one newly bereft and I—'

'She is heartbroken!' Mr Brontë, interrupting, emphasised. 'Distraught and dreadfully alone… desperate for the company of people with whom she can relate. People with similar interests… writing and such…'

'Quite…' Mr Nicholls concurred.

Mr Brontë retuned his gaze momentarily to the resting place of his daughter, and then sighing and shaking his head, he turned back.

'Alas, there's a limit that a father can do to alleviate

his daughter's suffering... convince her that some kind of future exists still,' he said and then in the next instant his demeanour brightened and he smiled. 'But never mind, Charlotte's friend will be here for her tomorrow. Ellen's company never fails to revive my daughter's spirits.'

Mr Nicholls' lips tightened and his eyes widened in a bewildering display of petulance, and he turned. 'Good day, Mr Brontë,' he said brusquely, as though stung, and then strode briskly away.

Mr Brontë, puzzled and shaking his head, watched, as the agitated curate strode determinedly toward the church door. After opening it, Mr Nicholls hurried outside, slamming the door noisily behind him.

Chapter Four

Pages of a manuscript were strewn across the dining-room table. Charlotte shuffled through them; she readjusted her spectacles and then lifted a page up to her eyes, while dragging the lighted candle closer. Squinting under its stuttering light, she struggled to make out the words, tiny words, written in her own hand some days earlier. After setting the page back down on the table, she picked up her pen and dipped it in the inkwell, but then glanced next at her father sitting dozing in a chair by the fire. Holding in one hand the crumpled pages of a newspaper, in his other, which rested on his lap, the magnifying glass that he used to help him read through eyes that, like the rest of his body, were succumbing to the ravages of the advancing years. A saucepan falling to the floor in the kitchen roused Mr Brontë and he looked fitfully about, before resting his tired, but contented, gaze with his daughter. Charlotte smiled, and then lowered her head. She scored out several sentences, writing different ones quickly and neatly in the space above. Her father, smiling fondly, allowed his eyes to close once again. But they were wide and staring in the next instant when the wind gusted, rising to a chilling screech that raised the hackles on the back of his neck. He sighed, folded up the newspaper, put it aside and set the magnifying glass down on top of it.

'Time I rested my head on my pillow,' he said, grimacing

and groaning as he shuffled toward the edge of his chair and heaved himself up.

Charlotte put down her pen.

'Sorry, Papa, did you wish me to read to you?'

'No, no, not tonight, Charlotte,' he said. 'There's little of interest in the newspaper today.'

Tottering unsteadily on legs stiffened from sitting too long, he bent down, picked up the poker and stoked the fire. He shovelled on more coal and tossed on another log. After straightening, he shuffled closer to his daughter, hovering over her and watching as she worked on her novel.

'Put no more fuel on the fire tonight, Charlotte, it will do now until you retire.'

'Oh, but I've no intention of retiring to my bed for a while yet.'

'You'll tire yourself... writing day and night—'

'Writing is not tiring, Papa, or I would not do it. Writing is a pleasurable occupation, an utterly relaxing experience, when I have a mind for it. Writing is cathartic...' she said and then smiled. 'People I like enjoy a happy life. Enemies suffer!'

Mr Brontë smiled. 'Well... you've not been in the best of health lately, and you still need to sleep.'

'Indeed I do, Papa, but my story comes effortlessly to me, and while it does I shall write the words down on paper before they are lost.'

'Ellen will be here tomorrow, don't forget.'

'Yes, Papa, I know she will. And my novel will not progress at all while Ellen is here.'

'Well... there'll be time enough to write another day,' he said, shuffling toward the door. He stepped from the room, turned and stood a moment, watching with pride as his studious daughter went about her work. 'Goodnight, Charlotte,' he said at last and then turned.

'Goodnight,' she called back, adding in her next breath, 'fret not for me, Papa, for I'll sleep easier tomorrow night when Ellen is here.'

'Then sit not long in the cold once the fire is out, for it's another bitter night,' he said, and then closed the door.

Charlotte removed her spectacles and listened for her father's footsteps on the stairs. The footsteps stopped, part way up the stairs by the alcove. The clock's ratchet turned, a dozen times or more, the case was snapped shut and his upward trudge resumed. Charlotte smiled; she replaced her spectacles and then lifted the page she had amended up to her eyes and read the words out loud.

Mr Brontë, shuffling on the landing and about to step inside his room, halted, angled his head and listened. He smiled and waited until Charlotte's voice fell silent, before stepping inside his room and closing the door.

Chapter Five

A knock on the parsonage door signalled the arrival of Charlotte's friend, Ellen Nussey. The two dogs, Keeper and Anne's spaniel, Flossy, were plunged into a frenzy, scurrying about and barking to rouse their deceased owners from their graves. The animals, though, were not the only ones propelled into a volatile state; Martha Brown, the Brontë family's young servant, raced excitedly out from the kitchen.

'Silence, dogs!' She yelled. 'Keeper, Flossy! Quiet!'

'Quit hollering, child!' Tabby, hobbling after her, shouted. 'You make more noise than those stupid blasted hounds.'

'Quiet!' Martha yelled again in defiance, glaring at the elderly servant who stood in the kitchen doorway, her arms folded across her breast, shaking her head and wincing each time Martha shouted at the dogs.

When the outer door was opened the young servant's demeanour altered abruptly and she smiled readily in an expressive, exaggerated manner.

'Miss Nussey…'

'My dear, Martha…' Ellen said, throwing her arms wide and gathering the young servant into them. 'How pleasing to see you looking well and healthy. Illness, I can see, has bypassed you!'

Martha nodded eagerly.

The coachman followed carrying Ellen's luggage. He deposited the suitcases on the floor in the hall and, after receiving his fare, bid the ladies good day and then departed. Ellen removed her coat and bonnet and Martha took them from her and hung them on the coat stand.

Tabby hobbled toward Ellen, beaming and wiping her hands on her pinafore.

'Ellen, my dear girl.'

'Dear Tabby... you, too, look in fine health... a healthy glow to your cheeks indeed,' she said, scrutinising the elderly servant after embracing her.

'Your cheeks would shine, Ellen, had you been standing aside the hot cooker all morning,' Tabby said. She hobbled away, wincing and rubbing her thigh. 'All that heat does nothing for my lame leg though.'

Footsteps sounded on the stairs and Ellen's gaze turned sharply upward, and then her face exploded with delight.

'Charlotte, my dear friend,' she said, hurrying toward her.

'Ellen,' Charlotte enthused, 'I'm glad you were able to come.'

The two friends embraced and kissed, and then Ellen, after taking Charlotte's hands into hers, stepped back and looked her up and down.

'Well, you appear nowhere near as ill and downhearted as I was led to believe from your last letter.'

'Knowing that you would be arriving soon revived me like you would not believe, dear Nell,' Charlotte said, darting forward and kissing her friend once again. 'Oh, Ellen...'

'Martha!' Tabby barked. 'Get to your work, child... standing gawping. Those suitcases won't climb the stairs by themselves.'

Martha turned to Tabby and scowled. She remained tight-lipped, but bent down and picked up the two suitcases and charged upstairs, battering them against the banister and the wall.

'Poor, Martha…' Ellen said, as she watched the young servant struggling. 'She's the strength of a man, nay a horse.'

Martha turned and neighed like a horse, and then giggled.

'Quit horsing around, child!' snapped Tabby.

Charlotte and Ellen both laughed and Tabby, unable to retain her stern expression any longer succumbed and smiled, but in the next instant the elderly servant's features hardened and she turned sharply to Charlotte and Ellen.

'And you two,' she barked, glaring, 'loitering in the draughty hall… go sit by the fire,' she ordered them, looking directly at Ellen. 'Charlotte's been laid up for much of the winter with one ailment following another—'

'You exaggerate, Tabby,' Charlotte said. 'A stubborn cold, the usual headaches and indigestion, that's the worst of it, but all will mend now that Ellen is here.'

'It won't mend if you're intent on hanging about all day in draughts,' Tabby snapped. 'The fire's blazing, go sit by it and I'll fetch you a mug of beef tea – a slice of bread and butter?'

'Coffee and biscuits, if you please, Tabby,' Charlotte said and smiled.

The servant looked sharply to her. 'You think I've nothing better to do all day than bake biscuits?'

Charlotte's smile widened. 'Thank you, Tabby,' she said. 'Life is infinitely sweeter and more pleasurable with you looking out for us.'

'And your cooking, Tabby…' Ellen began. 'Well, it would excite and delight Queen Victoria and Prince Albert's taste buds, I'm sure.'

Tabby beamed. But in the next instant her features altered and her ireful stare returned. Charlotte and Ellen looked to each other and giggled and then hastened into the dining room, settling onto the two chairs close by the fire.

Tabby entered not long after, carrying a tray with the promised mugs of coffee and a plate of biscuits. After setting the tray down on the table, she left the friends alone and they talked excitedly for half an hour and more, barely pausing for breath. The clash of the parsonage door closing silenced them both. First, the scuffing of dog's paws on the stone flags in the hall, followed by footsteps and then the rustle of clothing. The dining room door was pushed open, granting access to Keeper and Flossy and; as the dogs bounded toward Charlotte, Mr Nicholls shuffled into the doorway. Charlotte, after stroking the animals, smiled and looked up.

'I trust you are well, Mr Nicholls? The dogs well exercised?'

'Yes to both,' he replied, smiling excessively and then his lips stretched even wider and he turned to Ellen. 'I trust you enjoyed a comfortable and trouble-free journey, Miss Nussey?'

'Comfortable! I've been half-frozen, shook up and shaken about in a draughty carriage for half the day,' Ellen complained, looking sternly to him, as if he had been the instigator of her discomfort. 'The best that can be said, Mr Nicholls, is that the experience was a tolerable one: a necessary inconvenience in order that I could come and see my friend and nurse her back to rude health.'

Mr Nicholls' smile morphed rapidly, acquiring the bemused look of a schoolboy after being reprimanded for a minor but despicable indiscretion.

'Poor, Ellen,' Charlotte said, touching her friend's arm and smiling. 'Suffering so for my sake—'

'Yes, for your sake, Charlotte, and because I care.'

Mr Nicholls alternated his afflicted gaze from Charlotte to Ellen and then to the dogs, once they had returned to him. He bent down, stroked and patted the animals. On straightening, his smile returned and it was to Ellen he faced again.

'I trust you'll take care not to overtax Charlotte while you are here?'

'Overtax Charlotte!' Ellen exclaimed, affronted. 'I come here to see that she does not overdo it, Mr Nicholls, not to overtax her and make her unwell.'

'Quite...' he said, smiling uneasily. 'Forgive me, Miss Nussey, but I... I mention it only because Charlotte has been unwell for much of the winter, one illness following another and—'

'Thank you, Mr Nicholls,' Charlotte cut in. 'Ellen is a fine nurse and takes better care of me than I am able to myself.'

Mr Nicholls' smile widened. 'Then I'll bid you ladies, good day,' he said, nodding and gesticulating, calling the dogs to him, turning and then striding away.

Ellen glared after him but she remained silent and waited until hearing the parsonage door close, before turning to Charlotte, clearing her throat.

'Impudent man! When have I not taken good care of you?'

'Please do not be offended, Ellen. Mr Nicholls means well,' Charlotte said. 'Papa thinks highly of him and he's a useful man to have around, even if his manner is at times a little prehistoric.'

'At times, huh!'

'Mr Nicholls, I'm sure, sees in me a lost soul; a black sheep among his disciplined congregational flock, a free spirit in need of reigning in – of steering onto the path of righteousness.'

'Then beware the sentinel ram that might one day have a mind to entice his errant black ewe away from the flock... to dishonour her—'

'Ellen…! Mr Nicholls' interest rests only with my sisters' dogs. He likes nothing better than striding across the moors with Keeper and Flossy gambolling at his side.'

'The dogs, I suspect, are not all that Mr Nicholls would take to the moors, given the opportunity!'

'Honestly, Ellen… Mr Nicholls is Papa's pious curate, for heaven's sake!'

'No matter, he is of the male species and will take his chance like any other lustful lothario. If the dogs are his sole excuse for creeping about, stealing shameful looks then he fails to conceal it. Your father ought to remind Mr Nicholls of his duties, and if he strays from the path of righteousness, he should be sent back to Ireland.'

Chapter Six

Whether Ellen's suspicions had merit or not, the overzealous curate did, on occasion, exceed his pious and parochial responsibilities, which was evident some days later when Mr Nicholls returned the dogs to the parsonage one cold and drizzly afternoon. A look of horror widened his eyes when he saw Charlotte and Ellen in the hall, dressed in their coats and bonnets and about to step outside. It was to Ellen that he vented again his displeasure.

'Surely, Miss Nussey, as friend and supposed nursemaid to Miss Brontë, you cannot be thinking of allowing her out on such a foul afternoon?'

'Allow me out!' Charlotte cut in, exasperated. 'I am not a caged bird, Mr Nicholls, let out only for the entertainment of others.'

'No, no, of course not, but, but, I…' he stuttered, gesticulating uncomfortably.

'The fresh air, Mr Nicholls, even if light rain is in the air, will do Charlotte no harm at all,' Ellen stressed.

'And in any case we are walking no further than the baker's and the stationer's,' Charlotte informed him, taking Ellen's arm and smiling provocatively. 'And as you can see I am in expert hands, Mr Nicholls.'

Ellen's elevated head and her supercilious look, adopted specifically for the purpose of vexing Mr Nicholls, produced the desired effect and added to his displeasure. The irate curate nipped his lips tight together, turned and then stormed away. Charlotte and Ellen, struggling to keep their amusement in check, watched him leave.

'Good day ladies,' Mr Nicholls' retorted, yanking open the door, stepping outside and slamming it behind him.

Charlotte and Ellen broke into fits of giggles.

'Interested only in the dogs!' Ellen scoffed.

Mr Nicholls was right, though, the afternoon was not conducive to walking far. The rain was only light and the wind moderate, but it was bitterly cold day. Neither Charlotte nor Ellen appeared unduly concerned, though, linking arms and conversing, they skipped merrily along like schoolgirls stealing away from despised lessons. Calling first at the baker's, where Charlotte purchased bread and flour as a favour to Tabby, since she was "going out", as the servant had so eloquently decided. Charlotte's real purpose was to the stationer and the two friends' spirited entrance alerted the proprietor, Mr Greenwood, to the potential for profitable business. Appearing suddenly from behind a partition, rubbing his hands together, his face beaming.

'Ah, Miss Brontë,' Mr Greenwood began. 'I've neither seen nor heard from you in days – weeks! And I thought you'd taken your business elsewhere.'

'Never, Mr Greenwood.'

'Then, I trust my favourite customer has remained well during her absence?' He said, turning and glancing out of the window. 'It's a miserable afternoon to be out especially if you've been—'

'Before you say any more, Mr Greenwood,' Charlotte interrupted, 'I've suffered lectures enough today with regard to my health, being upbraided for ill-advisedly waking out in the rain.'

'Then I'll say no more, Miss Brontë, for it would be remiss of me to alienate my best customer.'

'Envelopes, if you please, Mr Greenwood, that's all I require from you today.'

The business conducted and the two friends stepped back out into the drizzly afternoon. The people they encountered contributed, inadvertently, to the time spent exposed to the rain, several of whom stopped to talk, congratulating Charlotte on her success. Some of whom were keen to know what she was currently writing, how many books she had sold, and the date that her next novel would be completed and published, its title, but more importantly, when it would be available to purchase in Mr Greenwood's shop.

Charlotte was a local celebrity and it was understandable that her adoring readers should wish to detain her and speak. She was admired and revered by many in Haworth and beyond, and was always happy to oblige them with a portion of her time and exchange a friendly word.

'Literary success, I see, has made you famous, Charlotte,' Ellen commented. 'You cannot walk down the street, even in the pouring rain, without being mobbed. Everyone knows you and everyone seems keen to stop and speak with you.'

'Well, why shouldn't everyone know me, Ellen? Haworth is a small community. I've lived here most of my life and know practically everyone. I have no enemies that I'm aware of.'

Once the rain had eased, Charlotte and Ellen decided to stretch their legs some more, extending their walk beyond the confines of the village in order to enjoy the fresh air while they were able. The afternoon had brightened considerably but it proved only temporarily. For, on reaching the edge of the moor, the clouds thickened and the rain returned, falling heavier than previously. Their spirits, though, remained undimmed; more agreeable company for either could be found nowhere in the world. The fresh air and exercise had done them no harm at all, and had sharpened the appetites of them both.

On approaching the parsonage, Ellen caught sight of a bedraggled figure dashing out from behind a tree, hiding behind a wall and peeping out from around it. She said nothing to Charlotte, but afforded herself a wry smile, for it seemed that the person who had earlier advised against pursuing the reckless adventure in the rain, had taken no heed at all of his own warning. Dressed inappropriately, Mr Nicholls had put his own health at greater risk than they, having evidently watched over Ellen and Charlotte every step of the way.

Neither Charlotte nor Ellen suffered any ill effects from the walk; their bonnets were soaked and their hair was wet, but their coats had kept their dresses dry. Fresh air and exercise was, as Ellen frequently advocated, necessary and beneficial in securing a healthy body, and a healthy body ultimately benefits one's mind. Indeed, a pink hue coloured Charlotte's cheeks and, purged of the waxen look that she had carried throughout the winter months, she not only glowed and looked healthier but appeared happier than for some time.

Chapter Seven

While Ellen stayed at the parsonage, Charlotte never added a sentence or a single word to *Villette*. She had neither the inclination nor the appetite for work while the company of her friend remained on offer. Not a minute was wasted; if the day was fine they took the gig into Keighley, visited the library, or attended functions at the Mechanics' Institute. Another day they might board the steam train in the town and travel to Bradford to enjoy the city, visit the museum or go shopping.

One day when the weather was especially warm and sunny they packed a picnic hamper and carried it onto the moors. Sharing the vast moorland with the birds, the rabbits and the sheep – and Keeper and Flossy. Upon reaching a high point, they secured a comfortable position and sat upon the soft heath sheltered from the wind, and on rocks warmed by the sun, and enjoyed their picnic, chatting and laughing like they were schoolgirls again.

'Mr Nicholls will be miffed…' Ellen said matter-of-factly, tossing a crust of bread to the dogs.

'Why on earth should Mr Nicholls be offended?'

'Deprived of his canine duties… but, on second thoughts he'll perhaps be displeased greater being denied the opportunity of feasting his eyes upon the love of his life.'

'Honestly, Ellen! Persist in your fanciful speculations, and I might be inclined to think you jealous.'

'Me, jealous! Never.'

Ellen stayed at the parsonage for a number of weeks and Charlotte remained healthy and happy for the entire time. Liberated from the rigours and the disciplines necessary for an author, her mind was free of the stresses brought about by the hours of intense concentration. The headaches and nausea she suffered were either of a mild affair, or banished completely; and she wished that Ellen could stay forever. But with her publisher pressing for the completion of *Villette*, Charlotte knew that she must work again someday soon, and Ellen would have duties of her own to her own family. Added to that it became necessary for Ellen to make way for the arrival of Mr Taylor, a representative from Smith, Elder & Co., Charlotte's London-based publisher. After attending business in Scotland, he had secured arrangements to call at the parsonage before returning to London. Wishing to see for himself the wild and rugged landscape that was the backdrop to Charlotte and her sisters' novels. Charlotte suspected a different motive, deciding that Mr Taylor had perhaps been instructed to call at the parsonage, by his boss, Mr George Smith, in order that it might speed up the completion of *Villette*.

Mr Brontë looked forward to meeting Mr Taylor, but Mr Nicholls was outraged.

'What can you be thinking, Mr Brontë? Are you out of your mind?'

'I beg your pardon!'

'Charlotte has only recently recovered from illness. Her constitution is not strong. You know it and yet you open your doors to all and sundry. Ellen has not long gone, and now Mr Taylor… I urge you, Mr Brontë, put a stop to his visit. Charlotte is not up to entertaining this… this endless procession of dubious visitors.'

'Dubious visitors! Charlotte's known Ellen since they were schoolgirls.'

'But Mr Taylor—'

'Mr Taylor is calling on business matters.'

'Business matters! Business is the duty of men, Mr Brontë, and you, as Charlotte's father, should deal with all matters pertaining to business.'

'Charlotte's writing is her business, not mine—'

'Charlotte has been weakened by illness; she is not robust enough to be troubled with the machinations of business. Furthermore, Mr Brontë, if you allow your daughter to cavort about the village on the arm of some slick stranger from London, unchaperoned, Charlotte will be ruined.' Mr Nicholls seethed. His entire body trembled. 'You ought not allow it, Mr Brontë!'

'Ought not allow it!' Mr Brontë repeated slowly, astonished and glaring. 'But, but what business is it of yours anyway?'

Charlotte appeared on the stairs at that moment, silencing them both. The dogs, excited by the furore fussed about Mr Nicholls' legs and he bent down, stroking and petting the animals. When he next looked up, Mr Brontë was shuffling hurriedly away toward his study, shaking his head. Charlotte stepped from the stairs and shot a puzzled look toward her father. Shrugging and smiling, she looked down upon the excitable dogs, and then faced Mr Nicholls.

'Your presence, it seems, is the dog's cue for exercise, Mr Nicholls. They become excitable at the sound of your voice.'

'Indeed, as I for your, for, for…'

'I beg your pardon, Mr Nicholls?' Charlotte entreated, perplexed and furrowing her brow.

'I, I… oh, no matter, Miss Brontë,' he mumbled, discomfited and gesticulating awkwardly. Grimacing, he turned away, clearing his throat. 'Keeper, Flossy, come. To the moors.' He turned back, forcing a nervous smile. 'I'll bid you good day, Miss Brontë,' he said and then strode away behind the boisterous dogs. He opened the outer door and stepped hurriedly outside, calling to the animals.

At that moment Tabby emerged from the kitchen carrying a tin of polish and cleaning rags. She jumped when the outer door slammed shut and turned sharply to it.

'What's gotten into him?'

'Oh, I do not know, Tabby,' Charlotte said. 'Men… they seem never happier than when trying the patience of us women.'

'Seems to me he's sickening for something else!' Tabby said, smiling knowingly, as she limped past. 'Martha!'

Martha bolted from the kitchen and charged across the hall and into the dining room, halting abruptly and scowling when Tabby forced cleaning rags into her hands. The elderly servant, after prising the lid off a tin of wax polish, stroked a cloth over it and then thrust the tin in front of Martha. The young servant, looking at the rags with disgust still, lifted up her head and faced Tabby.

'Well, take it, child,' she barked.

Martha compressed her lips, snatched the tin of polish from her and then loaded the cloth with a large dollop of wax, which she began smearing over the furniture.

Tabby glared. 'You've wax enough on your rag to preserve a fleet of ships for a century!'

Martha glared back, wiping petulantly the excess wax from the furniture onto her pinafore and then, after taking the cleaning cloth into both hands, she began polishing the furniture with exaggerated vigour.

Chapter Eight

Mr Nicholls, agitated and breathing heavily, darted from one doorway to the next; he charged across the street, peeped around the corners of buildings, dived behind bushes and looked through the branches, all the time keeping his distance, and out of sight from Charlotte who walked out in the village on the arm of Mr James Taylor. The curate's wounded eye, focussed firmly upon the pair, failed to notice the bucket that someone had left lying in the street. He stumbled over it and in a rage kicked it away, leaping from sight a split second before Charlotte and Mr Taylor turned round.

Rage contorted Mr Nicholls' face when Mr Taylor whispered something in Charlotte's ear that made her laugh out loud. Grinding his teeth and screwing up his fists, the curate seemed poised to break cover and challenge the publisher for his too liberal ways with Charlotte, but he took a deep breath…

'Might they become lovers?' Mr Nicholls asked Tabby the next morning. 'And do you think Charlotte might be in love with Mr Taylor?'

'You'll learn nothing from me,' snapped Tabby. 'Even if I was intimate with her thoughts,' she said, brushing the curate aside and shuffling past.

'But has, has Charlotte taken breakfast yet this morning?'

'Shout her! Ask her yourself. Charlotte! Charlotte! Mr Nicholls–'

'Sshh, Tabby!' He pleaded, waving frantically to her. His agitated manner excited the dogs; Flossy scurried about his legs and almost tripped him up and Keeper jumped up at him and almost knocked him over. 'Down, Keeper, down!'

Charlotte appeared on the stairs.

'Did you wish to speak with me, Mr Nicholls?'

'I, I… yes, no, but I…'

'Yes or no? Which is it to be?' Charlotte said irritably, as she breezed by him and continued into the dining room. Mr Nicholls, flustered and gesticulating followed.

'Well…?' Charlotte, facing him, asked.

'For-forgive me, Miss Brontë, but as your father's servant, and friend. I feel it is my duty to warn you that, that man is no good for you.'

Charlotte's eyes widened. 'By *that man* I presume you mean Mr Taylor?' She said, exasperated. The curate nodded, uneasily. 'Then, pray, Mr Nicholls, please explain the reason for your warning.'

'I, I—'

Footsteps in the hall curtailed his faltering reply and Mr Nicholls' lips tightened with outrage when Mr Taylor, dressed smartly in a suit and tie, strode blithely into the dining room. His eye shot straight to Charlotte.

'Miss Brontë, a very good morning to you, my dear,' Mr Taylor said cheerily, greeting her with unexpected familiarity and taking hold of her hand, lifting it up to his lips and kissing her fingers, to Charlotte's exasperation. Aware suddenly of the presence of another, he turned sharply.

'Ah, Mr Nicholls! A very good morning to you, sir. I trust you are well?'

'Tolerably so,' he replied bluntly and then in his next breath and without conviction, asked, 'Yourself?'

'Fine, my good man, fine,' Mr Taylor said, turning back

to Charlotte. 'As is the weather, Miss Brontë. A fine morning for a stroll, I rather thought. I wonder, perhaps you'd like to escort me to the moors and introduce me to the wild and rugged landscape I read of in your novels.'

After a further expression of outrage, an overstated smile came suddenly to Mr Nicholls' lips.

'If exercise is what you desire, Mr Taylor, perhaps you'd like to accompany myself and the dogs on the moors, good sir.'

'No, no, Mr Nicholls,' Charlotte cut in. 'That will not do at all. I'll not have *you* put out by *my* guest.' Smiling, she turned back to Mr Taylor. 'And besides, Mr Taylor and me have important business matters to discuss, haven't we, James?' She added provocatively.

'Business… ah, yes,' Mr Taylor said and laughed. 'Yes, yes, of course.'

Mr Nicholls, unable to disguise his displeasure, flashed a piqued glance toward Mr Taylor, and then stormed from the room.

'Keeper, Flossy!'

The clash of the parsonage door signalled Mr Nicholls' departure. Mr Taylor, frowning and shaking his head, turned to Charlotte.

'Strange man…'

'Oh, Mr Nicholls carries out his duties well enough,' she said, and then turned to her father who, at that moment shuffled into the dining room, looking somewhat bemused.

'Was that Mr Nicholls leaving?'

'It was, Papa.'

'What reason is there for slamming doors at this hour – at any hour for that matter?' Mr Brontë said, before turning to Mr Taylor and smiling. 'James, my good man… sad to hear it, but I believe you'll be leaving us in the morning?'

'Indeed, I'm afraid I must, Mr Brontë.'

'Must?'

'It's abominable to flee yours and Charlotte's company so soon, I know, but an overseas adventure awaits, and I cannot delay another day.'

'Well, perhaps Charlotte might like to accompany you to London?' Mr Brontë said somewhat hopefully, turning to his daughter and smiling encouragingly. Mr Taylor smiled.

'Papa!' She protested. The abruptness of her tone displaced Mr Taylor's smile, and with it any optimism he may have had in securing Charlotte's company on the train journey to London.

'Well... she is busy with her novel,' Mr Brontë offered by way of an excuse. 'But when you next visit, Charlotte will perhaps have grown tired of writing... and be ready for settling down with a husband.'

'Papa!' Charlotte protested again, more vociferously than before, glaring at her father. 'I'll be forty in a few years' time, and Mr Taylor will not want an old maid for a wife, I'm sure.'

Mr Taylor shrugged. Mr Brontë's lips tightened and he shook his head. Charlotte excused herself and hurried from the room.

*

Ellen Nussey had visited and gone. Mr Taylor had been and concluded his business – if any at all had indeed been conducted – and had returned to London. Charlotte was alone once again. Another morning and the same dreary routine began, accompanied with the usual attacks of nausea and headaches from the moment of awakening: breakfast, writing until midday; a break for dinner followed by more writing in the afternoon, varied perhaps, by a walk into the village, or onto the moors if the weather was fair; tea, more writing, and then, of an evening, reading to her father from the newspaper. It was while reading to him on one such evening that Charlotte noticed her father's eyes begin to close and reopen, and when they remained shut she halted.

'Papa?'

Mr Brontë started. He opened his eyes, yawning and stretching. 'The parish authorities continue to drag their feet over drinking water and sanitation issues.'

'You've said that twice tonight already, Papa,' Charlotte said, folding up the newspaper.

'Well, I raise the subject time and again with the committee, plead with them to deal with the matter with the utmost urgency, but to no avail.'

'Committees!' Charlotte scoffed. 'When was anything ever achieved by a committee? People attending committee meetings spend all their time drinking tea and eating biscuits, drinking gin and deciding on the date of the next committee meeting.'

Mr Brontë looked sharply to her, but he chuckled and shook his head. When he stood up, Charlotte threw the newspaper aside and rose from her chair. She removed her spectacles, put them on the table and went to his aid. Taking an arm, she guided him toward the door.

'What a pity Mr Taylor had to leave so soon,' he said. 'Fine man—'

'Fine man nothing, papa!' Charlotte responded with unexpected venom. 'You know nothing at all of Mr Taylor.'

'I… I worry for your future.'

'Well Mr Taylor will not be part of it,' Charlotte said firmly. 'I thought well enough of him at first, but the longer

I spent in his company, the more I grew to loathe the odious little man.'

Mr Brontë shook his head. Charlotte let go of his arm on reaching the foot of the stairs. She stood and watched him struggle up the steps, smiling when he stopped by the clock in the alcove.

'Goodnight, Papa,' she said, turned and walked away.

'Goodnight, Charlotte,' he called down. 'Sit not late… tiring yourself writing late into the night.'

Charlotte returned to the dining room and settled in her chair by the fire. After putting her spectacles back on, she picked up several pages of her manuscript and read from them out loud. The sentences, though, jarred and sounded disjointed. Sighing protractedly, she cast the pages aside, took a sheet of writing paper and picked up her pen.

"Dearest Nell,

Mr Taylor stayed only a few days, thank God. He is pleasant enough to do business with, but no more. Papa thinks well of him and sees him as a potential son-in-law! The thought brings on increased nausea. Mr Taylor will never do for me, not if he was the last man on earth. You may think me disrespectful and unkind, but the more I saw of the little man the more I resented him. Mr Taylor possesses an uncanny physical resemblance to Branwell and a union with him would to me seem almost incestuous. He makes my blood run cold, and now I cannot stand him near me for more than a few minutes – and he seems always predisposed to stand as close to me as he can, and at every possible opportunity. Thankfully, he will have left for foreign shores by the time you receive this letter. Hopefully, I will not need to deal with him anymore. I go to London on Monday for a welcome break from writing, Manchester the week after…"

Chapter Nine

Over the next few weeks Charlotte became involved in a pleasurable, if exhausting, social whirl, staying first in London at the family home of her publisher, Mr George Smith. He escorted her around the city, took her to the shows, to the opera, to the galleries, to The Great Exhibition, and to lectures given by Mr William Makepeace Thackeray, where, afterwards, Mr Smith introduced her to the celebrated writer.

When she tired of London, Charlotte travelled to Manchester and stayed at the home of the writer Mrs Elizabeth Gaskell and her husband, William, a church minister. Their four girls took instantly to Charlotte, and she to them, so when Mrs Gaskell attended other duties, the children kept her suitably entertained and Charlotte in turn entertained them with stories conceived at will from a fertile mind. From Manchester she travelled to Birstall, staying at the family home of her friend Ellen Nussey, her sister, Mercy and their mother. In familiar, friendly company Charlotte was able to relax completely, banishing the excitement and the stresses of meeting eminent new people in London. In Birstall all thought of work was put from her mind and she was free to enjoy walks in the fresh air in the solitude of the countryside with Ellen. The visit, though, was kept brief, as Charlotte, after being away from home for several weeks, became increasingly anxious to know how her father was. Troubled with bronchial infection, he was seldom in the best of health and she knew that he would worry for her and would be uneasy until she was safely back home.

Mr Brontë, though, was not alone in yearning for Charlotte's safe return. Mr Nicholls had, on a number of occasions, tested Tabby's patience, pestering her for knowledge of the day when Charlotte was expected to return home – information that she was unable to provide him with.

But Mr Nicholls, and indeed everyone, had not long to wait; the steady clatter of horses' hooves on the cobblestones in the lane was the precursor to settling anxieties. Martha heard it first and raced up to the window and looked out; she saw the horses and coach approaching and then ran from the room.

'Miss Charlotte's back! Miss Charlotte's home!' Martha shouted, as she raced through the hall toward the door. She opened the door and charged outside, jumping down the steps and skipping along the garden path. 'Miss Charlotte!'

Charlotte, disembarking from the coach, turned round and smiled seeing Martha open the garden gate and step out onto the cobbles. The servant, after embracing Charlotte, stood before her, smiling with child-like admiration.

'Well, you, at least, sound in fine voice, Martha?'

The servant nodded eagerly, and looked to Charlotte through widening eyes.

'Fame takes you everywhere, Miss,' she said. 'You've been away an age and everyone thought you were never coming back home.'

'Well, I am here,' Charlotte said, throwing her arms wide and embracing the servant girl again. 'But tell me, Martha, how is Papa? Indeed, where *is* Papa?' She said, shooting a glance toward the parsonage, and then looking about.

'With Mr Nicholls. He's been fair worried he might never see you again.'

'Papa thought—!'

'No... Mr Nicholls.'

'Mr Nicholls, but...'

Mr Nicholls and Mr Brontë emerged from the church together. They meandered in the direction of the parsonage engaged in lively, but amiable conversation. They had not walked far when Mr Nicholls, almost choking on his words, looked up and pointed, his face breaking into a smile. 'Horses and a carriage outside your home, Mr Brontë! Can it really be—?'

'Charlotte,' Mr Brontë cut in. 'God has taken care of my daughter and has delivered her safely home.' His relief was palpable, even if he was equally happy for her to tour the country, meet and socialise with people from all walks of life. He faced Mr Nicholls with a telling smile. 'Travelling does Charlotte much good, but it's always pleasing to have her safely back home. Her life these days seems one long whirl of socialising: London one week, Manchester the next, taking the sea air with Miss Wooler in Hornsea, visiting Ellen in Birstall.'

Mr Nicholls' features hardened. 'If you ask me, Mr Brontë, your daughter spends more time away from home than is good for her.'

'Nonsense,' Mr Brontë said, looking sternly to him. 'Visiting friends helps her to forget. And Ellen's company is better medicine than any poison doctors might prescribe.'

Mr Nicholls remained unconvinced. 'London, Manchester, Birstall... all unhealthy places for a woman born and bred in the country.' Piqued, he turned abruptly. 'I'll bid you good day, Mr Brontë,' he said, and then strode away in the direction of his lodgings.

'But, but will you not come... oh, do as you please,' Mr

Brontë uttered, bewildered and shaking his head, watching as the irate curate continued on his way.

The instant Charlotte heard the parsonage door close, she charged out from the dining room and into the hall, into the welcoming embrace of her father. Mr Brontë, unable to contain his delight, kissed his daughter's head and her cheek several times, and then he held her at arms-length, and with a widening smile, scrutinised her.

'A healthy glow indeed,' he said. 'But tell me, did you accomplish all that you planned? Did you go to The Great Exhibition? Attend the Thackeray lectures? Go to the opera? See Mrs Gaskell?'

'All of that, Papa, and then I travelled to Ellen's home and stayed with her for a few days.'

'And is Ellen and her family well?'

'Indeed they are, Papa, very well.'

'Well, you are home… but, what of the Exhibition? Was it all you expected?'

'My first thoughts were one of disappointment – of a street bazaar in a hot country – but on the second day I visited I decided it was something to be marvelled at: a wonderful display of all the things created by human endeavour.'

'And did you get the chance to speak with Mr Thackeray?'

'Indeed, I did. Mr Thackeray, well… he is huge, a great big bully of a man; twice my height, brash and rude. You'll not believe it but he wickedly introduced me to his mother as little Jane Eyre, can you believe! The worst of it was, he and I were standing in the middle of a crowded room and his voice boomed loud – everybody turned and stared and laughed. Mr Thackeray received the sharp end of my tongue for his mischief, I can tell you.'

Mr Brontë smiled, as did Tabby and Martha who looked

on from the kitchen doorway, listening to every word. Father and daughter then gravitated toward the dining room, when Charlotte stopped suddenly and turned.

'Tabby, Martha – refreshments, if you please. Make haste and then come and sit with Papa and me in the dining room and listen to the adventures of my travels.'

Martha, overawed and staring, watched as Charlotte and her father disappeared into the dining room. Tabby glared at the young servant.

'Well, look sharp about it, child.'

Martha, instead of exhibiting her usual display of petulance, raced into the kitchen, exhilarated, and Tabby, equally animated, hobbled hurriedly after her.

Charlotte guided her father to his chair by the fire and, after assisting him into it, sat opposite.

'Lily has the most wonderful—'

'Lily?'

'Mrs Gaskell has the most wonderful husband. They live in a large, fine house and every room is scented with the fragrance of fresh flowers. They are blessed with the most delightful children: four beautiful, healthy girls. Julia, aged five, is the youngest; she is truly adorable and you should see how her tiny fingers cling to my hand, and my dress. But each girl is pretty in her own way... intelligent and entertaining: Marianne is the eldest, next is Margaret and then Florence. I confess I cannot help feeling more than a little envious.' She halted suddenly and looked about. 'But where is Mr Nicholls? Martha said that he was with you.'

'Oh, he—'

'Is he well?'

'Well enough, I dare say,' Mr Brontë said, with a dismissive backhanded gesture. 'But never mind about him...'

The two servants, after carrying refreshments into the dining room, dragged a couple of chairs closer to the fire and sat, drank coffee and ate biscuits, while listening to stories of Charlotte's adventures; of how Mr Smith's mother was sometimes disapproving of her, and was especially discourteous when she and Mr Smith returned home late after visiting The Great Exhibition. Mrs Smith accused her of dallying purposely with the intention of leading her son astray.

Martha's greatest joy was in listening to stories of Manchester. Charlotte's face illuminated all over again when she retold the stories of Mrs Gaskell's four girls, of how each had taken instantly to her; how the children had sat mesmerised when she told them tales of strange and wonderful people living on the moors about Haworth.

Once the stories of Charlotte's travels were done, the servants returned to their work; Martha, excited still, worked energetically and with newfound enthusiasm, to the astonishment of Tabby.

Charlotte remained with her father by the fire; she picked up the newspaper, opened it out and was about to read, but then noticed that his eyes were already closed. When she cleared her throat, he opened his eyes and looked to her.

'Shall I leave the newspaper until another day, Papa?'

Grunting something unintelligible, and with a backhanded gesture he signalled his willingness to concur. Charlotte smiled, folded up the newspaper and put it aside, stood up and went to him. Taking an arm, she helped him from his chair, steadying him when he tottered.

'Thank God your novels have reaped you financial success, Charlotte, and you now no longer need to rely on me for your living,' he said and sighed. 'I struggle with the simplest tasks these days. Once I could walk up and down the steep hills about our home and think nothing of it, but getting out of my chair is now a trial. I fear the day when I'll no longer be here is not far off.'

'Speak not so, Papa! That day is many years away, I'm sure,' she said, stroking her father's arm reassuringly, as she guided him toward the stairs.

'I can manage now,' he said, grumpily, upon reaching them. But he smiled and his tone softened. 'Sit not late, Charlotte, for it's another cold night and the fire burns low already.'

'But I must write, Papa, I promised Mr Smith—'

'Promises, huh? There'll be time enough to write another day.'

'I dare say there will, but I've been idle for too long. I must curb my wandering spirit, or *Villette* will never be finished,' she said, and then disappeared inside the dining room.

Charlotte dragged a chair closer to the dying fire and sat down. She put on her spectacles, reached out and grabbed her shawl from the back of the chair and wrapped it around her shoulders. Her father was right: it was a cold night and she had a mind to shovel more coal onto the fire but, conscious of her father's fear of being roasted alive in his bed after Branwell one night set fire to his bed sheets, she dismissed the thought the instant it had entered her head.

Chapter Ten

Visiting friends and socialising were not the only obstacles to the completion of *Villette*. Influenza had infected many people in the village and those living in the Brontë household were not immune.

Tabby hobbled into the dining room one morning, coughing, sneezing and sniffing, wafting a duster futilely over the furniture. Charlotte, sitting at the table, busily writing her novel, looked intermittently to her, tightening her lips and wincing each time the servant coughed or sneezed. Then, when Tabby, groaning and moaning after dusting the mantelpiece, shook the cloth by the fire, drawing out a plume of smoke that set them both coughing, Charlotte slammed down her pen.

'For heaven's sake, Tabby, leave the dusting. Go and make yourself a hot drink and take it with you to your bed.'

'I'm paid to work and I'll work if it kills me.'

Charlotte removed her spectacles. 'I'm liable to kill you, Tabby, if you will not please do as I ask and leave the dusting.'

The servant slumped in a chair and began polishing the table legs. 'You'll think me worthless and be rid… employ a younger girl in my place.'

'We'll do no such thing, Tabby. You've been with us an age – indeed you are part of our family. Now, please do as I ask. Martha's in the kitchen, tell her what needs doing, she'll finish any cleaning.'

Reassured, Tabby smiled. She stood up and limped away, groaning and rubbing her thigh. Charlotte replaced her spectacles and picked up her pen and; left undisturbed, sentence after sentence flowed and soon another paragraph had been completed, and then another and before long *Villette* was another chapter closer to completion.

Optimism that her novel might be finished over the coming weeks, though, was dashed when her father shuffled into the dining room one evening a few days later, coughing, sneezing and wheezing. With his illness any hope of completing *Villette* over the coming weeks ended abruptly: the needs of the sick took precedence over all else. And after running up and down the stairs all day, caring for her father – worrying about her father – Charlotte had barely the strength to climb them of an evening, let alone clear her head and apply her mind to writing.

'My pistol, Charlotte!' Her father demanded, as soon as she set his bedtime mug of warm milk down on the bedside cabinet.

'Papa...' she began, sighing resignedly, yielding to his request nevertheless. 'Must we continue to suffer the violence of that thing firing each morning?'

'We must,' he replied. 'It's not safe to leave a loaded pistol about the house all day. The bullet must be discharged.'

'But is it really necessary to have a loaded gun about your person anymore? The threat from the Luddites passed years ago.'

'I dare say it has. But who can tell what vagabonds and cutthroats roam the moors these dark winter nights?'

Once the pistol was loaded and slipped under his pillow, Mr Brontë smiled, reassured that he could sleep safe in his bed for another night. Afterwards, Charlotte sat at her father's bedside and read articles to him from the newspaper, as he sipped his warm milk. When the mug was empty, and her father had snuggled lower beneath the sheets, she stopped reading, put down the newspaper, stood up and tucked the sheets tight about him. She leaned over and began plumping up his pillows, when he sneezed.

'Go, Charlotte! Leave me,' he bid her, easing her gently away. 'Do what you must and avoid this, this... ah, ah a-choo.'

'I'll fetch the doctor.'

'No, no, Charlotte, I'm in need of no poisoning doctor. Leave me,' he urged. 'Go... remove your presence from this room before you, too, are infected.'

She retreated as far as the door, from where she stood watching and waiting until the sneezing had subsided. When he at last relaxed and had closed his eyes, she opened the door quietly and exited.

After making herself a mug of coffee, Charlotte took a couple of biscuits from a jar and retreated into the dining room. She slumped in her chair by the fire, staring abstractedly into the dancing flames as she chewed on a biscuit and sipped coffee, but with little appetite for either. Conscious, though, of the need to force some nourishment inside her weak and exhausted body in order that she might refuel it in readiness for another day of similar toil tomorrow. The hot drink soothed her and the warmth of the fire made her drowsy and, after putting aside the empty mug, she fell into a deep sleep. She awoke some hours later in total darkness, cold and shivering; the candle had burned out and the fire had died. She stood up and fumbled a route to her room with only the starlight to guide her. It was cold in her bedroom and colder in her bed and she suffered an uncomfortable night. Nightmares arriving with terrifying vividness, violating what precious moments of snatched and fitful sleep she was able to achieve.

The following morning, hunched and bleary-eyed, Charlotte descended the stairs to the galling sounds of coughing and sneezing, both upstairs and down. Worse awaited her, though; she entered the kitchen to find, Martha stirring the pan of porridge, sneezing and sniffing.

'Oh no, not you now, Martha!' Charlotte cried resignedly.

'I'm real sorry, Miss,' the servant girl said, turning. 'But I can't help it I—'

'Bed, Martha, this instant!'

'But porridge'll burn if I don't keep stirring, Miss—'

'Leave it, Martha, I'll see to the porridge. Go home and ask your mother to make you a hot drink, and then go straight to your bed.'

Mr Nicholls bounded energetically up the steps toward the parsonage door. The door opened and Martha dashed out, pulling a scarf up over her mouth. She glanced to him but hurried past without speaking.

Puzzled and frowning, Mr Nicholls turned and watched the young servant hurry away. Shaking his head, he turned back and stepped inside, closing the door quietly behind him. Hearing noises in the kitchen, he smiled and meandered in that direction. He looked set to step inside, but halted seeing Charlotte bent over, stirring the porridge pan. His smile widened, and he resisted the temptation to speak straight away and stood there watching but then the patter of dogs' paws on the stone flags in the hall turned Charlotte's head. She gasped, clutching her breast.

'Mr Nicholls!'

'For-forgive me, but I—'

'I did not hear you enter,' she said, and then smiled. 'And I was unaware that I had an audience.'

'I, I—'

'Well you at least seem yet in good health, Mr Nicholls?'

'To be sure, Miss Brontë, but with much influenza about the village, I fear it will infect me sooner or later.'

'Sooner, I should say, if you choose to linger in this unhealthy household. I've only this minute sent Martha home.'

'Yes, yes,' Mr Nicholls said, turning to the dogs that jumped excitedly about his legs. He bent and stroked and patted the dogs. 'Come, hounds, we must take heed of your mistress's concern and escape to the moors… fill our lungs with the sanitised moorland air.' After pausing, he smiled. 'Don't neglect the porridge, Miss Brontë.'

Charlotte smiled, and then returned her attention to the porridge pan. Halting abruptly and turning back, but Mr Nicholls had disappeared.

'Roam not far,' she called out to him, turning back to the porridge pan. 'It's much too cold out today.'

Mr Nicholls poked his head back round the kitchen door and stood smiling in admiration as Charlotte stirred the porridge, and then he crept quietly away.

'Good day, Miss Brontë,' he called back, and then opened the outer door.

The dogs charged outside, Mr Nicholls followed them and then closed the door. He stood a moment on top of the steps, looking out from the elevated position, filling his lungs with the fresh morning air. Smiling broadly, he descended the steps and strode briskly away, calling the dogs to him.

Burdened with the household chores, cooking, shopping, cleaning, washing and caring for the sick – fretting over her father's worsening health – it was inevitable that Charlotte's health should suffer. Headaches became excruciating and nausea obliterated her appetite completely. She grew weak and anaemic and, unsurprisingly, her spirits sunk. Sitting alone of an evening, her depression deepened and it was in those quiet and reflective moments that her thoughts turned inevitably to her siblings; to the cruel, bleak winter months when one by one, her brother, Branwell, and then her sisters, Emily and Anne succumbed to the same deadly consumptive illness and perished. The nights now, as then, were unbearable and Charlotte was kept awake by the echo of endless coughing, and by the groans of the sick; and sleep, were she able to secure any at all, came only with the new morning, and by then it was too late.

When it seemed that the deepest part of the pit had been reached, from where things could only improve, Mr Nicholls, after calling to collect the dogs one morning for their daily walk on the moors, returned only minutes later carrying Emily's dog, Keeper, in his arms. Old age had caught up with the animal and the dog failed to see out the day. With Keeper's passing another chapter of Charlotte's life was closed, awakening with it painful memories: images of Emily charging over the heathland with Keeper gambolling at her side, and of her sister goading the animal until it bared its teeth, in a cruel test of its loyalty to her.

Next, when Charlotte felt that she needed her friend, Ellen, most it became necessary to cancel a planned visit. It was then, when exhausted and at her lowest ebb that Charlotte, too, succumbed to the influenza virus.

Chapter Eleven

Now it was Charlotte's turn to be nursed and Tabby, herself recovered, fussed over her charge like an over-attentive mother: pressing a cold hand to her patient's forehead and checking her temperature; taking hold of Charlotte's wrist and timing her pulse; scalding her for leaving the mug of beef tea she had made for her untouched; and if Tabby detected the slightest shiver, she procured more blankets and heaped them onto her bed.

'Tabby, please!'

'I'll fetch my thick nightgown, that'll keep you warm—'

'I'll not wear it, Tabby,' Charlotte protested. 'I'm boiling hot as it is!'

'You've a fever! Sweat it out. That's what my grandmother always told me – she swore by it.'

'I'll swear, Tabby, if you don't, well…' Charlotte began, halting and sighing resignedly when the servant hobbled hurriedly away.

Tabby returned promptly carrying yet more blankets, throwing them on the bed and spreading them out and, from a pocket in her pinafore, she pulled out a cold wet cloth, which she pressed against Charlotte's forehead.

'For heaven's sake, *Granny*, let me alone – please,' she pleaded, flipping over in her bed like a petulant child.

'Lie still, will you!' Tabby admonished, attempting to reapply the cloth. She was unsuccessful, though and stood over Charlotte, shaking her head and frowning. 'Were I your grandmother I'd tether you to the bedposts, stop you frigging about one way or another. Ellen will be here in a day or two and heaven help me if she thinks I've been neglecting you.'

'Ellen will think no such thing, Tabby. She knows you are capable.'

When Charlotte's friend Ellen Nussey did arrive no one was more pleased, or relieved to see her than Mr Brontë. The minute she stepped inside the parsonage, the empty stare that he had carried for days was gone, his brow appeared less wrinkled and the days of distracted ruminations were brought to an end.

'Ellen,' he said, beaming, as he embraced her. 'Thank God you were able to come. Charlotte's been laid up for days. She is indeed fortunate having a loyal, caring friend.'

'And is Charlotte very ill, Mr Brontë?'

'The fever has abated somewhat, but she's troubled now with a worrying cough and—'

'Then let's hope and pray it's nothing worse than a nasty cough.'

'Indeed.'

Ellen removed her coat and bonnet and hung them on the coat stand, and then headed straight for the kitchen. Mr Bronte, following close behind, began to divulge to her every symptom and detail of Charlotte's illness.

'Beef tea, if you please, Tabby,' Ellen said, after greeting the two servants.

Only then, when equipped with the necessary information, and a mug of Tabby's beef tea, did Ellen ascend the stairs. She entered Charlotte's room and found her friend asleep, buried almost from sight beneath sheets and pillows. After setting the mug down on a bedside cabinet, Ellen elevated her head and sniffed the air, in what might be perceived a condescending manner, and then she strode purposely toward the window. The noise of it being forced open roused Charlotte from her slumbers and she peeped cautiously out from beneath the covers, breaking into a smile the instant she saw her friend.

'Ellen… I thought for a moment I was dreaming still!'

'Charlotte, my poor, dear friend…' Ellen, said, dashing to her bedside. She folded back the sheets, nipped her lips together and looked her over. 'Hmm, your father said you were drained and withdrawn, and I'm inclined to agree. But you look nowhere near as ill and downhearted as I'd been led to believe. The worst is over and you will get better now I am here.'

'Oh, Ellen…' Charlotte said, and then coughed, protractedly and for some minutes, before being able to continue. 'It's been a trial caring for Papa with Tabby laid up and Martha at home sick.'

'Well, the servants, thank God, are much recovered, but your father looks a little pale and weak still.'

'Fretting over my health, I'm sure, has impeded Papa's recovery. Indeed he and Tabby have been beside themselves with worry, and were set to fetch the doctor tomorrow, were you unable to come, Ellen.'

'Doctors have their uses…' Ellen said, somewhat dismissively. Leaning over Charlotte, hoisting her up from beneath the sheets and arranging several pillows behind her back, propping her against them. 'Right… now I can see you, I can decide what's to be done.' She pressed a hand against the patient's forehead.

'Ah… a warm hand…'

Ellen looked sharply to her. She took hold of Charlotte's hand, upturned it and placed two fingers on her wrist and checked her pulse.

'You have a temperature still, for sure, but your pulse remains strong. And your cough... well, perhaps the apothecary will have some linctus that will cure it – let's hope!'

Charlotte smiled. 'I'm afraid you'll find me poor company, Ellen.'

'Poor company!' Ellen repeated, looking sternly to her. 'I'm not here to be entertained, Charlotte, I'm here to make you better.'

Charlotte smiled. 'The worst of being ill is the inconvenience of it... of lying in bed and unable to do a thing. I've not written a single sentence in ages. *Villette* has lain untouched now for weeks, and Mr Smith presses—'

'Mr Smith!' interrupted Ellen sternly. 'Mr Smith will wait.'

'To be sure, Ellen, but I cannot neglect my work forever and must write again one day soon or *Villette* will never be finished.'

'Mr Smith cares nothing for the Charlotte Brontë that I care about. Mr Smith cares only for Currer Bell and the fortunes *he* can bring. Be assured, Charlotte, for as long as I am here *Villette* will remain untouched. You need complete rest, and rest is what you'll have. Now, drink the beef tea Tabby has made for you before it goes cold.' Charlotte lifted the mug up to her lips and took a tentative sip. 'All of it.'

Ellen sat on the bed and the two friends talked while Charlotte drank the recuperative beverage. After draining the mug, handing it to Ellen and lying down in her bed, her cough returned: a nasty, chesty cough that seemed would never stop, leaving her exhausted when it did. Ellen then lowered the pillows, straightened the covers and tucked the sheets tight about her friend, and when Charlotte closed her eyes, she crept quietly away and out of the room.

Mr Brontë was waiting. Pacing anxiously about in the hall, a concerned and shuffling figure but then he heard Ellen's footsteps on the stairs. He looked up and smiled.

'Well, Ellen… your prognosis?'

'Nourishment and rest, Mr Brontë, that's what Charlotte needs,' she affirmed, stepping past him and progressing into the kitchen. Tabby and Martha looked sharply to Ellen, startled by the abruptness of her entrance and by her authoritative tone.

'Nourishment and rest, Ellen?' Mr Brontë repeated, shuffling behind her. 'Nothing more?'

'Nothing more, Mr Brontë,' Ellen stressed. She turned to him and her tone hardened. 'But she'll get no rest with greedy publishers pestering her to write more money-spinning novels, and as soon as Charlotte is fit to travel, I'm taking her to Birstall. At my home she'll not be hounded by people eager to swell their fortunes from the toil of others.'

'An admirable recommendation, to be sure, Ellen,' Mr Brontë agreed. 'But her appetite is poor and I fear it'll be some time before Charlotte is fit to travel. You'll find she'll eat little or nothing at all.'

'Eat little or nothing, Mr Brontë!' Ellen repeated slowly, exasperated. 'If Charlotte contrives to take little or nothing at all, she'll have food forced down her throat.'

Mr Brontë smiled, reassured that his daughter was at last in capable hands. He turned and shuffled from the kitchen, his smile widening with each step as he headed toward his study. It widened further hearing Ellen issuing instructions to the servants – instructions that the servants were willing to undertake, it has to be said – confident in the knowledge that, under Ellen's supervision and care, Charlotte would recover in little time. He stepped into his study with the music of pots and pans and cutlery, and

Ellen's voice in his ears. After closing the door, he sat down at his desk and took out several papers from a drawer, but they remained unread on his desk for some time, while he sat listening. Charlotte, he knew, would be restored to rude health in little time.

Chapter Twelve

Charlotte's health had improved significantly, but she was still not fully recovered when Ellen took the decision to take her to Brookroyd, to her family home in Birstall. Ellen decided that a change of air and removal from Haworth, beyond the reach of her publisher, was the tonic that Charlotte needed.

The January morning was perfect for travelling; after a frosty night, the air, though cold, was fresh and the sun beamed welcome, if insipid, warmth upon them from an alluring cloudless sky. The two friends took the gig into Keighley, from where they caught the train to Leeds. From Leeds they procured a carriage that conveyed them on the last leg of the journey to Birstall. The instant the horses and carriage drew up outside Ellen's home, her sister, Mercy, raced out from the house to meet them. Greeting Charlotte with hugs and kisses, before turning and embracing Ellen and then bidding them both hurry inside and out of the cold.

Having stayed at Brookroyd many times before, Ellen and Mercy were now like sisters, substitutes for the ones that Charlotte no longer had, and Mrs Nussey could hardly have shown greater affection had she been Charlotte's biological mother. As soon as Charlotte stepped inside, Mrs Nussey came dashing into the hall, fan in hand, kissing and fussing over her in her customary overstated manner and then she helped take off her coat, handing it to Mercy to hang up.

'Come, Charlotte,' she urged her, ushering her into the living room. 'Neglect not your health… loitering in draughty halls,' she said and then turned. 'We must take care, Ellen. Make sure Charlotte is kept warm at all times, and not let her go wandering about the cold countryside, as she is apt to do.'

Ellen was neither reckless nor disrespectful of her mother's wishes, but she was an advocate of fresh air and exercise and possessed an astute sense of what was good and right for Charlotte. And it should have come as no surprise, least of all to Mrs Nussey, that, on the second morning into Charlotte's visit, she should find her and her daughter in the hall, dressed in their outdoor attire and about to venture outside.

'Dear me, Ellen, what can you be thinking?' She protested. 'Risking the life of a famous writer!'

'Mama, the sun is shining.'

'Indeed it's a beautiful morning, Mrs Nussey,' Charlotte concurred. 'And it would be a shame to waste it; better to take advantage while we can, for who can tell when the sun might next shine.'

'But, but…' Mrs Nussey stuttered and in a fluster she flew to a window and looked out. 'Clouds, big black clouds, waiting on the horizon,' she said on returning, shivering exaggeratedly. 'It feels like snow to me, Ellen.'

'Mama, it always feels like snow to you,' Ellen mocked. 'But where's the harm in taking a short walk while the sun is shining?' She tugged at Charlotte's coat. 'Look, see Charlotte is wrapped up like a Christmas present.'

'My concern, it seems, is fit only for your entertainment,' Mrs Nussey complained. 'Be it on your head, Ellen, if Charlotte should fall ill again.'

'Please do not concern yourself for my sake, Mrs Nussey,'

Charlotte cut in. 'Ellen is a fine nurse. Indeed it is due to her expert nursing that I am now much better.'

'Then I'll say no more,' Mrs Nussey said, sniffing and sighing, opening out her fan. 'I caution only against taking unnecessary risks with the life of the famous Currer Bell.'

'To you, Mrs Nussey, I had hoped to remain always Charlotte Brontë.'

'To me you'll be no other,' Ellen said. 'Only death can change our friendship.'

'I pray, then, that such a day is many years away,' Mrs Nussey said, fanning her face. 'And I pray also that no harm befalls Charlotte Brontë because of the recklessness of my daughter.'

'Pray also, then, Mama, that the snow keeps away until we are safely back home,' she said and laughed. Mrs Nussey's lips tightened in outrage. Ellen tugged at Charlotte's arm. 'Come,' she urged. 'Let's escape while we are able. Before Mama procures a rope and tethers us to the table legs.'

Ellen's amusement continued and Charlotte laughed, if somewhat cautiously.

'Laugh all you will,' Mrs Nussey said, working her fan fast and erratic in front of her face. 'But don't say I didn't warn you.'

Ellen opened the door and the two friends escaped into the January sunshine. It was a pleasant enough morning, and especially pleasing to feel the sun's warmth on bodies that had been denied its beneficial properties for much of the cold winter months. The sunshine and exercise warmed them in little time, and Charlotte appeared relaxed and happy, as indeed did Ellen. However, the two friends amid cordial, and at times, spirited conversation neglected to take notice of the distance they had walked, or of the rapidly darkening sky.

Clouds that had not long since seemed anchored securely on the horizon appeared overhead and hid the sun. Charlotte and Ellen, immersed as they were in frivolous moods, seemed not to notice the sun's absence – or perhaps did not care. Endeavouring to push or pull each other onto the ice-capped puddles that littered the path, giggling and screaming as they danced around the icy patchwork, like the insouciant schoolgirls that they long since once were and Ellen teased Charlotte.

'Your publisher, you say, speaks fondly of you, and I believe he will visit you soon? Might he propose?'

'I rather think not, Ellen,' Charlotte replied. 'Obstacles would undoubtedly be put in his way should he aspire to any such reckless undertaking. After thinking once well of me, Mr Smith's mother ages half a century should I have the audacity to glance upon her precious boy for more than half a second. She, for one, would not grant permission, nor, I suspect, would his sister. Mr Smith is visiting only to see if Currer Bell is fit for work. Mr Smith's interest rests only with the fortune my books bring him and his publishing company. As far as Charlotte Brontë is concerned, Mr Smith is as blind as a bat. Marriage, my dear, deluded friend, has passed me by.'

'What, then of Mr Taylor! He will one day return from India—'

'Stop it, Ellen, matchmaking is not your forte.'

'And I harbour no such pretensions, but make mere observations, that is all.'

'Then your observations are misguided, and in any case you already know my thoughts concerning Mr Taylor. I know not when the *little man* will return from India and care even less. So please, dear Nell, spare me the trauma of attempting to match me with men who are unsuitable – undesirable.'

Ellen's eyes widened. 'Well, if all else fails there's always Mr Nicholls!'

'Ellen…'

'Deny it if you dare, but more than once I have seen the keen eyes of your father's curate ravishing you – mentally perhaps – but, unless you are blind, you must know it to be true, also…'

'No man could be more unsuitable than Mr Nicholls, Ellen. I should die of boredom were I to strike up a relationship with as dour and dull a man as he. In any case Mr Nicholls is already married – to the church – to his submissive and pliable flock.'

Ellen and Charlotte laughed and they continued in silence for a while, immersed in thoughts of their own, when Ellen halted suddenly and seized hold of Charlotte's arm.

'We must hasten home immediately,' she demanded, looking anxiously up to the snow that had begun to fall. 'Mama will be furious if I return you home looking like a snowman.'

'Me, a snowman! For the life in me, Ellen, I fail to see how a flurry of snow might possibly promote the growth of testicles,' Charlotte said and laughed.

Ellen was livid.

'Make not light where your health is concerned, Charlotte!'

'Ellen… I am well enough now,' Charlotte assured her, struggling to speak amid her laughter. 'A snow shower will do me no harm at all.'

Charlotte's amusement continued, and Ellen finally succumbed and giggled, and then the two friends turned, linked arms and hurried homeward, each supporting the other along the slippery path.

'Honestly, Charlotte, is that the kind of vulgar language you pick up walking the streets of London?'

Ellen's concern, though, was understandable; Charlotte seldom enjoyed good health. Headaches and nausea had troubled her for much of her life; her constitution was not robust and seemed a magnet for every illness. Of greater urgency right then, though, was the snow that fell heavier in the strengthening wind.

Chapter Thirteen

Mrs Nussey was frantic and distraught, staring in disbelief out through the window at the falling snow. After stepping away, she paced about the room, dashed back and then turned to Mercy, who was sitting reading on the sofa. Her features twisted and hardened.

'Why didn't you stop them, Mercy? You heard me didn't you? You heard me tell them it would snow, didn't you? But did you stop them?'

'Mama…' Mercy said. 'Charlotte and Ellen will be fine.'

Mrs Nussey was not convinced. She turned back to the window and pushed her face close to the glass panes, turning this way and that, looking in every direction for signs of her daughter and Charlotte. She remained there, fanning her face, for some minutes, sighing, periodically berating her daughter, and then the pitch of her voice rose all of a sudden.

'Mercy!' She cried out. 'Dry towels, quick! Fetch dry towels. Poor Charlotte, she'll be frozen half to death.'

Mercy threw her book down on the sofa and stood up.

'What about poor Ellen?'

'Never mind about your foolish sister – warm dry clothing, and quickly, and the fire!' She blurted, snatching the poker off its stand, jabbing it repeatedly into the coals. She shovelled on more coal, threw on more logs, and then rubbed her hands together, dashing the dirt from them before wiping them clean on her dress.

Mercy returned with towels and found her mother agitated still, dashing in one direction and then another, stepping to the window and waving frenziedly to Charlotte and Ellen, urging them hurry. She turned back to the fire, picked up the poker and attacked the coals once again and shovelled on yet more coal.

'For heaven's sake, Mama, calm your temper before your brain explodes. Charlotte will be fine, you'll see.'

Mrs Nussey was anything but calm and, after throwing the poker down on the hearth, she charged into the hall, opened the door wide and stood resolute in the snow that blew inside and upon her.

'Come, come… hurry,' she called out, beckoning them with repeated frenetic waving. 'Didn't I tell you?' Mrs Nussey raged, looking to Ellen, but taking hold of Charlotte's arm and half dragging her inside. 'Didn't I say we'd have snow? But would you listen?' She closed the door, shutting out the snow and the wind. 'Look at you both… like a pair of red-nosed snowmen!'

Charlotte and Ellen looked to each other and giggled.

'And it amuses you, does it? Does it?'

'Mama, you excite yourself over nothing,' Ellen said.

'Nothing! Nothing!' Mrs Nussey was incensed, pulling the gloves from Charlotte's hands and rubbing her fingers. 'You poor woman, how you suffer—'

'I suffer nothing, Mrs Nussey, honestly. Now please…' Charlotte pleaded, freeing her hands.

'Take your wet garments off at once,' Mrs Nussey demanded, turning to Mercy and snatching the towels from her. 'Come, Charlotte, take heed, take these, and take yourself off upstairs and dry yourself. Ellen, give Charlotte a good rub.'

Mercy chuckled. 'Do not bully her, Mama. Poor Charlotte…'

'And the fire, Mercy! Give it another poke, and more logs—'

'Mama!'

'Dear me, my foolish daughter, putting the life of the famous writer, Charlotte Brontë, in mortal danger.'

'Mortal danger nothing, Mama… but yes, you were right, the snow did fall,' Ellen conceded. 'But look, see the pink glow about Charlotte's cheeks. Anyone can see that she has come to no harm at all.'

After removing their coats and bonnets, hanging them to dry, Charlotte and Ellen took the towels and then fled upstairs. They returned soon after to find the drama playing still. Mrs Nussey was waiting for them in the hall and she pounced the instant Charlotte stepped from the stairs, seizing her arm and harrying her into the living room. Once inside, she insisted that Charlotte sit on the chair closest to the fire.

'Dear me, Mrs Nussey,' Charlotte complained, cooling her face with the motion of a hand as she sat. 'You are indeed kind, but if I remain this close to the fire for more than a few minutes I shall be crisp and brown like a roast chicken.'

'Please do not mock, Charlotte – it's enough that Ellen should poke fun. I do it for your own good only.'

Charlotte smiled. 'Then please do not be offended, Mrs Nussey; I jest only to try and lighten your mood. We must all find time for fun in our lives, for no one can be certain what the next day might bring. Fret not for me; Ellen is indeed a fine nurse and possesses an uncanny knack of knowing instinctively what is best for me. Yes, we were dismissive of your advice; we paid the price and were caught out by the snowstorm. But I honestly believe that the fresh air and exercise – Ellen's excellent and agreeable company – has done me much good.'

Mrs Nussey adopted a despairing mask and then slumped down on the sofa; she opened out her fan and fanned her face.

'Then my nerves have been tried for nothing,' she said, working the fan faster.

Charlotte was right, though, Ellen's instinct, where her health was concerned, was seldom amiss and recovery from illness seemed almost guaranteed, and if Ellen's care was the medicine that restored Charlotte to rude health, then her friendship was the necessary stimulant that lifted her spirits from the mire of depressive gloom.

Unfortunately Charlotte was unable to stay forever and, after being from home for over two weeks, her thoughts began to turn to her father. Added to that was the need to return home and work, complete *Villette* and silence Mr Smith.

A knock on the door signalled the end of Charlotte's recuperation. Mercy invited the coachman inside and pointed out Charlotte's luggage. He nodded, picked up the suitcases and exited with them, despite Mrs Nussey's voluble plea to him to leave them where they were, while in the same breath begging Charlotte to extend her stay.

'You'll be much better in another week,' she pleaded.

'You are indeed kind, Mrs Nussey, but I'm sufficiently recovered and I really must return home and work.'

Mrs Nussey would have detained Charlotte forever had she been able. Defeated, she fussed over Charlotte instead, adjusting her clothing, checking and double-checking that she had everything she needed in order to make the journey as safe and comfortable as possible. She thrust a thick blanket into Charlotte's arms, insisting she take it to protect her knees from the cold while travelling and a heavy shawl to keep the drafts from her neck and shoulders.

'If only you could stay longer—'

'Were I able, Mrs Nussey, I would stay forever, but I must return home and finish my novel, and Papa will be anxious to have me home again.'

'Then write to Ellen,' Mrs Nussey implored. 'Write at every opportunity and keep us informed. Put our minds at ease and send for Ellen at the first sign of illness,' she said, as she attempted to spread the shawl over Charlotte's shoulders.

'For heaven's sake, Mrs Nussey, let me alone, please,' she pleaded, snatching the shawl from her. 'I am quite capable of dressing myself.'

'And do not tire yourself writing day and night,' Mrs Nussey cautioned. 'For if word reaches that you've been over doing it, I'll despatch Ellen right away to separate you from your work... worrying us half to death, as you seem determined to do. You must make your publisher understand that your health comes first, Charlotte. Tell Mr Smith that you'll not be rushed.'

'Worry not, Mrs Nussey,' Charlotte said, embracing her.

'Seeing how ill you were when you arrived, worry we most certainly will.'

Charlotte and Ellen walked arm in arm toward the awaiting carriage, happy and conversing, even though they were sad at parting. They embraced and kissed and then Charlotte climbed on board. She settled into her seat and covered her legs with the blanket, and spread the shawl over her shoulders.

'Thank your mother again for the blanket and shawl, Ellen,' Charlotte called out. 'I'll return them when I next visit.'

'And make it soon, Charlotte.'

The driver closed the coach door. He climbed on board

and sat in position, picked up his whip and cracked it over the horses' backs and called to them to move on. The two animals snorted their defiance, shook their heads and then staggered forward.

The two friends blew kisses and waved, and Mrs Nussey and Mercy, standing outside the door of their home, waved, too, as the coach moved slowly away. All stood waving and smiling until the carriage had disappeared from view and then their faces assumed a look of sadness. Ellen, her sister and mother turned and sauntered back inside their home. Life, they knew, would seem dull by comparison until Charlotte visited again.

Chapter Fourteen

A storm raged outside; it was wet and wild and the wind's mischief seemed almost to have sneaked inside, stalking about the rooms like an unwelcome guest, chilling all that it touched. Charlotte shivered and pulled the shawl she wore – Mrs Nussey's shawl – tighter about her shoulders, looking instinctively to the window when an angry torrent was dashed violently against the glass panes. Sighing, she removed her spectacles and stared out into the blackness: *The representation of her future*, she wondered. *Bleak and empty; drowning under an endless deluge of misery and heartache, of loneliness.* Using a fold from her dress, she cleaned her spectacles and then put them back on. She picked up her pen, dipped it in the inkwell and wrote.

Minutes later her father shuffled into the room, breaking her concentration.

'Toiling late again? Persist, and I'll be forced to send for Ellen,' he said, with a look of playful severity, before glancing to the fire. 'Put no more fuel on tonight, Charlotte. It's wild night again, but better that we freeze to death than be burned alive in our beds as we sleep.'

'Worry not, Papa, the fire will have gone out long before I'm done.'

'Then sit not in the cold once it is out,' he said. Standing in the doorway, watching his daughter writing. When she looked to him, he smiled. 'Well, goodnight, Charlotte,' he said, and then turned and shuffled away.

'Goodnight, Papa.'

After winding up the clock in the alcove on the stairs, he progressed toward his room and was about to enter, but halted on hearing Charlotte's voice. Smiling, he angled his head and listened.

'Thousands weeping, praying...'

Charlotte's voice fell silent and Mr Brontë stepped inside his room and was about to close the door, but halted once again and listened.

'"A thousand weepers, praying in agony on waiting shores, listened for that voice, but it was not uttered."'

Mr Brontë's smile widened and he closed the door.

*

The days and nights of endeavour generated its ultimate reward: *Villette* was at last finished. But the usual burst of euphoria that accompanied the accomplishment of a protracted enterprise was this time absent. Had Emily, Anne and Branwell been alive, or even just one of her siblings, Charlotte's joy, her sense of achievement in completing another novel, would have meant so much more. But they were gone from this life and it was futile to dream.

Unable to sleep, Charlotte rose early the next morning. After breakfasting, she procured a sheet of brown paper and a length of string and wrapped and bound her manuscript. She was about to secure the string when the door opened and Flossy sauntered inside, wagging his tail and sidling up to Charlotte.

'Flossy,' she uttered, smiling fondly and then knotting the string. She picked up her pen, dipped it in the inkwell and wrote the name and address of her publisher on the parcel. Scuffed footsteps in the hall halted her, drawing her eye toward the door. The door opened.

'Mr Nicholls…'

'Hard at work again, Miss Brontë?' he said, disapprovingly.

'Indeed, it is the end of it, Mr Nicholls,' she said, smiling generously, before finishing writing the address on the parcel. '*Villette* is done, wrapped up and ready to be posted to my publisher.'

'Finished!' Mr Nicholls repeated, his frown mutating into a smile that stretched wider than Charlotte's. With brightening, smiling eyes he shuffled closer to her. 'You'll now perhaps find time to pursue other interests?'

'I dare say I will – must – or loneliness will be my lot for evermore.'

'Flossy, come. To the moors,' Mr Nicholls said, turning and practically dancing from the room.

Bemused, Charlotte stood watching, shaking her head.

Mr Nicholls was right, though, she thought; now that her novel was finished it was imperative that she found some other absorbing activity to occupy her time. Something that would engage her mind and help quell the rumblings arising from the void left in the wake of extinguished lives. She could, of course, begin another novel, but…

After checking that the manuscript was securely packaged, she picked up the parcel and carried it into the hall. She knocked on the door of her father's study and entered. Mr Brontë, bent over his desk, holding the magnifying glass over a page of the bible, turned.

'Charlotte….'

'*Villette* is finished, Papa.'

'Finished!' He uttered, shuffling round in his chair,

smiling. 'And does Paul Emanuel return safely from his voyage to the West Indies? And does Lucy Snowe continue to prosper with her school? Does she marry Mr Emanuel and live happy ever after?'

'Dearest Papa,' Charlotte said and laughed. 'You and Mr Smith are so alike – dewy-eyed romantics.'

'Well... there's sadness enough in this world, Charlotte—'

'I dare say there is, Papa. Sentiment is all well and good, but my novel is intended as a reflection of real life, and life, as you know, is not one long fairy story. The meagre amount of happiness we are able to secure is ultimately swamped, overwhelmed by suffering and heartache. All life ends with death: it can never end happily...'

'With God's will—'

'With God's will Emily would be alive still, so would Anne and Branwell, Elizabeth and Maria, and dear Mama – I wish that she had lived and I had known her...'

Mr Brontë sighed. 'We must be thankful, Charlotte, and not blame God for taking them from us.'

'No... but if just one of my sisters, Emily or Anne, or better still both were with us still, finishing another novel would mean so much more.'

'Alas, it cannot be...'

That which should have given cause for jubilation, for celebration seemed muted and devalued. A cloud of gloom descended, diminishing, or smothering the joy that would otherwise have been gained after successfully completing another novel.

Charlotte exited her father's study feeling utterly wretched. She encountered Tabby in the hall and their eyes met. Yet, despite her sadness, and the overwhelming sense of injustice she felt at being deprived of her siblings and her mother, Charlotte summoned the will to smile. Tabby reciprocated, returning a generous smile, a warm smile that shone through her sometimes obdurate manner. The servant remained a formidable presence in her life still; and when her spirits were low she knew that she could always rely on Tabby to impart some semblance of enlightenment, one way or another. Mr Nicholls was right, though, Charlotte again thought; now that her novel was finished, the void must somehow be filled.

Chapter Fifteen

Lonely cold winter nights were spent huddled by the fire, writing letters or reading. Reading articles from the newspaper to her father, but he was in his bed by nine o'clock and Charlotte sat alone, pondering the bleak and lonely future she envisaged. Ahead she could see only solitude and memories; empty long days and sleepless cold nights. She looked at the clock and sighed; the evening was young still and with no novel to write, she seemed destined to suffer another lonely night – a night of silence and torment.

It was a wild night; a blizzard raged, the wind wailed. It groaned ominously inside the chimney breast like a trapped beast, and then its spirit broke free and spilled out into the room in its smoky guise. Charlotte coughed and shivered; she put on her spectacles and picked up the letter she had received recently from Ellen. She scanned the letter and then put it back down, shuffled to the edge of her seat, stood up and stoked the fire; she shovelled on more coal and threw on another log. Stretched her legs and walked to the window and looked out upon the virulent night, wondering at the business of a person in the lane. Sighing heavily and, with an anguished expression, she returned to her chair by the fire and sat back down. She took hold a sheet of writing paper and picked up her pen…

"Dearest Nell,

Warmest thanks for your kind invitation. I should very

much like to visit, but first I must travel to my publisher's office in London and correct the proofs of Villette…"

Snow had fallen steadily throughout the day and several inches covered the ground, and still it fell, emptying the streets of all but the hardiest of souls, or desperate persons on an urgent mission – or fools. In the lane outside the parsonage, stood a person befitting one such description: a man, a man on a mission of some kind; an anonymous man, his features concealed behind an upturned collar and a scarf, hunched and nervous, shuffling his feet in the ankle-deep snow. The blizzard seemed the last thing on his mind. He stood rubbing his hands together, looking fitfully about and then his demeanour altered all of a sudden. He opened the garden gate and strode purposefully along the path, over the undisturbed snow toward the parsonage.

Candlelight flickered in the un-shuttered window of Mr Brontë's study, and the ageing parson shifted labouredly into view. He stood in front of the window and looked out upon the falling snow. The man, mid-flight midway along the garden path, stopped; he tugged at his collar and stood watching and waiting; and then when Mr Brontë moved away, the man continued toward the parsonage. He climbed up the steps and formed a fist and was about to knock on the door, when the dog barked. Unnerved and irritable, he turned and descended the steps quickly but carefully, and then hid from view around the side of the building.

Mr Brontë reappeared in the window in an instant, pistol in hand and waving it about. He opened the window and leaned out, pointing his pistol from one point to another.

'Who's there?' He called gruffly out. Only Flossy responded, yapping and growling behind him. 'I'll set my dog on you,' Mr Brontë threatened, glancing down upon the harmless spaniel at his heels, and then he looked outside once again, standing there and looking about for some minutes more, before closing the window. He retreated, but remained uneasy and paraded back and forth in front of the window, before sitting back down in his chair, keeping the gun within easy reach on his desk. He picked up the magnifying glass and held it over the already opened bible and read, glancing periodically to the window.

The man emerged from hiding, trembling from the cold or from fear – or both – it was impossible to tell. Angry and dejected, he walked briskly in the direction he had come, but then halted abruptly, rebuked himself, turned around and strode determinedly back toward the parsonage. He climbed up the snow-covered steps and this time, without hesitation, and despite the dog barking again, he knocked on the door, opened it and hurried inside, closing the door after him.

Flossy pounced straight away, barking excitedly and jumping up about his legs, as he wiped the snow from his boots on the doormat. The commotion drew Tabby out from the kitchen.

'Mr Nicholls! What in heaven's name!'

'Parish business, Tabby.'

'Parish business! Well, I'll be surprised if Mr Brontë's expecting you tonight with a blizzard blowing. It's a cold and miserable night to be out,' she said and then turned abruptly from him. 'He's in his study.'

'Thank you, Tabby,' he said, somewhat distracted, deep in thought and wiping his feet on the doormat still.

Tabby, hobbling toward the kitchen, turned back round and with a stern stare looked down upon the curate's busy feet, and then she elevated her gaze until her eye was level with his.

'Wear that mat out, Mr Nicholls, and I'll take a pair of scissors to your beard and fashion a new one from your bristles.'

Mr Nicholls forced a smile and then stilled his feet. He brushed the snow from his coat and then stepped from the doormat; he took off his coat, his hat and scarf and hung them on the coat stand to dry, before shuffling hesitantly toward Mr Brontë's study. Sensing that Tabby's eye remained with him still, he turned back, smiled, knocked on the door and then hurried inside.

Mr Brontë turned sharply round.

'Mr Nicholls! What—?'

'Parish business.'

'Parish business! It's a foul night to be out. The business of the parish could have waited until another day.'

'Indeed, Mr Brontë, but I, I—'

'Oh, very well,' he grudgingly conceded, sighing. 'Close the door and come and sit down. The Lord will crucify me had I a mind to send you straight back out into the arctic,' Mr Brontë said, watching and waiting while the curate was seated, when his features hardened suddenly and he looked sternly to him. 'I trust you've not taken to bad habits, Mr Nicholls, and think to call at the Black Bull on your way home?'

'No, no, most certainly not, Mr Brontë!'

Mr Brontë closed his bible and pushed it aside. He pulled open a drawer and then took out a handful of papers. After setting them down on his desk, he fingered through them. Selecting several pages, which he examined through the magnifying glass, and then cleared his throat.

'Well, matters concerning sanitation and clean drinking water remain un-addressed still. The Board of Health have so far done nothing at all,' Mr Brontë declared, bringing his fist down hard on his desk, causing Mr Nicholls to jump. 'I

74

bring it up time and again with the committee but they do nothing about it. It's time people in authority got off their backsides and addressed the issues that matter to the public. Too much time has been wasted already. People are drinking contaminated water and are becoming ill: people are dying from want of clean water. The matter needs dealing with urgently, before, be—' Mr Brontë halted, noticing his curate gazing distractedly about the room. 'Do you listen to a single word I say, Mr Nicholls?'

'For-forgive me, Mr Brontë,' he began uneasily. 'But I, I can't help wondering what Charlotte will do now? What will occupy her time now she has finished writing her novel?'

'Charlotte!' Mr Brontë said, bemused and frowning. He scratched his head and stared hard at Mr Nicholls. 'I dare say she'll rest her brain awhile, and then perhaps write another novel. But such matters are of no concern of yours. Now, can we please get on with the business of the parish? That's what you're here for, isn't it?'

'Indeed… but I, but forgive me, Mr Brontë, if I—'

'What now?'

'Forgive me if I… if I encroach on matters that are of no business of mine, but it has not escaped me that Charlotte strikes a rather solitary figure. She is alone and I, I wondered—'

'Alone! *I* am here for her.'

'Indeed, Mr Brontë, but—'

A knock sounded on the study door and both men turned. The door opened and Martha, carrying two mugs, entered.

'I beg your pardon, Mr Brontë, Mr Nicholls,' she said, curtseying awkwardly, before facing Mr Brontë and smiling. 'But Miss Charlotte said you had a visitor… said he might need warming with a mug of beef tea. It's a cold night, Mr Brontë.'

75

'Indeed, it is a cold night,' Mr Brontë agreed, and then smiled. 'Thank you, Martha. Set the mugs down on my desk, if you please.'

She placed a mug on the table, one in front of each man, curtseying again and flashing a nervy smile toward Mr Nicholls, before backing slowly away, dawdling, alternating her gaze between the two men.

'Thank you, Martha, that will be all tonight,' Mr Brontë said.

Martha smiled and hurried from the room, closing the door quietly behind her. Mr Nicholls sighed. He picked up the mug in front of him and sipped from it and then set it noisily back down. He reached out and took the papers from the desk, the ones that Mr Brontë had earlier studied and, after skimming over the content, he threw them back down on the desk.

'I absolutely agree, Mr Brontë. If drinking water is not cleaned up, and quickly, cholera and typhoid will establish their evil presences, and be assured, more deaths will follow. People in the village are drinking infected water and they do not know it. It's time someone was booted up the proverbial—'

'Yes, yes,' Mr Brontë said, looking briefly to him, before drawing Mr Nicholls' attention to another issue on a different paper.

Together they worked through the parish business, discussing and analysing, sometimes in animated manner, arriving always at a unanimous agreement – Mr Nicholls agreeing with Mr Brontë, that is. And, engrossed, as the two men were, in the business of the parish, it almost seemed that Mr Nicholls had forgotten the reason he had braved the inclement weather to walk to the parsonage in the first place.

Chapter Sixteen

Charlotte, sitting close to the fire writing a letter, paused and turned thoughtful while looking affectionately to Flossy stretched out on the rug, when the dog's eyes flipped open suddenly. His ears pricked up and the dog sprang to his feet and raced to the door, barking and growling.

'Flossy! Come back here, boy,' she said, slapping her thigh.

Flossy obeyed, sauntering reluctantly back to her, but the dog's uneasiness remained and he growled periodically. Charlotte put down her pen, stroked and soothed the agitated animal. But scuffed footsteps outside the dining room door reignited the dog's excitement. A timid knock followed and she looked sharply to the door, bewildered and frowning.

'Enter,' she called out, standing up, and hurriedly straightening her attire.

The door opened.

'Mr Nicholls!'

'Miss Brontë, I…' he uttered, closing the door quietly behind him, before turning and facing Charlotte. He shuffled closer to her; his lips moved and it appeared that he would speak, but words failed him and he stood before her with quivering lips, looking directly at her through fitful eyes, stroking his beard and fingering his face and, despite the cold weather, beads of sweat appeared on his brow and stood proud like raindrops on glass. His breathing was laboured and he shifted constantly from one leg to the other, and at times he appeared to be on the brink of collapse.

'Are you unwell, Mr Nicholls?'

'I, I'm well enough, thank you, Miss Brontë, but I... but I've...' he mumbled, and then stuttered and stopped as his nervous gaze shifted between Charlotte and Flossy and back. He steadied himself and cleared his throat. 'I have borne sufferings, Miss Brontë, sufferings that I—'

'Speak up please, Mr Nicholls,' Charlotte cut in, frowning. 'For I can barely make out what you say.'

'I've nursed feelings for, for... and borne suffering I can endure no longer, and prayed, hoped that my—'

'Mr Nicholls!' Charlotte exclaimed, her eyes widening in astonishment.

'Hoped that my feelings might one day be reciprocated.'

Charlotte, standing rooted to the spot, gulped hard and stared in disbelief. Her un-shifting gaze discomfited Mr Nicholls and he turned away, looking distractedly about the room.

'But have, have you spoken with Papa?'

'I wished it but dared not.'

'Then you must leave, Mr Nicholls.'

'But, but I—'

Charlotte advanced toward the door and opened it.

'You know you cannot have my answer until Papa has been consulted,' she said firmly, holding the door open. 'Please leave, Mr Nicholls.'

Dejected, his head drooped and he shuffled disconsolately from the room, but he turned back abruptly and jammed a foot inside the door, preventing Charlotte from closing it.

'Will, will your father's blessing be given?'

'I cannot know that,' Charlotte snapped. 'Please remove

your foot, Mr Nicholls and leave, for if Papa should find you here, your wish most certainly will not be granted.'

Reluctantly, he withdrew his foot and Charlotte closed the door. She leaned with her back against it and stared straight ahead, clutching the doorknob so tight that her fingers turned white. Breathing exaltedly, her breast heaved and her eyes were wide and flitted restlessly about the room. Her lips quivered and parted; it seemed that she might break into an exhilarating smile or scream her joy to the world. She did neither, but waited until her fevered brain had cooled and then she stepped away from the door. Her heart, though, would not be tamed and continued to thump hard and erratic inside her breast.

A beacon of hope had been ignited and its flame burned with searing delight, with vacillating optimism, perhaps; but the more she thought about Mr Nicholls' proposal, the fiercer and more certain the flame seemed to burn. It burned so hot it scorched her heart: passions that had lain dormant or suppressed, waiting perhaps for the right moment, for the right man, burst inexplicably into existence.

Charlotte meandered unsteadily toward the fire and sat down in her chair. She closed her eyes and dreamed. She dreamed extravagantly and of a brighter future, of a future that offered the possibility of at last securing some semblance of emotional fulfilment, a release from her sorrows after the months and years of suffering; of a future with promise, with hope.

Chapter Seventeen

With a gladdened heart, but with a siren screaming its warning inside her brain, Charlotte stepped from the dining room and into the hall. A man had declared his love for her and she wanted to shout her joy to the world, but was uncertain how the world might react. She meandered about outside her father's study, her lips moving to the script as she rehearsed the lines of the drama in performance inside her head. *Papa, Mr Nicholls came to see me before leaving... Papa, Mr Nicholls wished to speak with you this evening on a matter of, of... Dearest Papa, did you know that Mr Nicholls was seeking a wife?*

Charlotte inhaled deeply; she held her breath and then knocked on the study door, exhaling with similar potency as she hurriedly stepped inside and closed the door.

'Charlotte!' Her father blurted, startled by the abruptness of her entrance.

'Papa...' She began, turning to him. 'Before Mr Nicholls left, he sought my company—'

'Did he indeed!' Mr Brontë barked. 'For what purpose?'

'He, he seeks a wife—'

'I knew it!' He retorted, jumping to his feet and slamming the magnifying glass down on his desk. 'I knew Nicholls was up to something... walking out in a blizzard under the pretence of parish business.' He stepped nearer to Charlotte. 'Confounded scoundrel, I trust you turned him down?'

'I did not.'

'You accepted!'

'I did not accept either,' Charlotte added. 'I merely intimated that I must speak first with you.'

'Speak with me! Why, when you already know my answer?'

'Had I known your answer it would have been given... but why this, this unwarranted outburst? I never saw you look so disagreeable, believed that you could be so unjust, nor hear you speak so bitterly of another to the point of vindictiveness. And never, not in my wildest dreams, could I ever have imagined that a harmless proposal would put you into such a rage.'

'Harmless proposal!'

'I dared hope... think that you might have been pleased for me, for until this moment I have only ever heard you speak well of Mr Nicholls.'

'Aye, as my curate, not as, a, a... the Judas!'

Mr Brontë's body trembled: his eyes bulged, his face reddened and the veins at his temple stood proud and pulsated hard and fast and it appeared that they might explode and spill blood. Charlotte dared not say another word from fear of provoking a seizure, and then, when her father began gasping for breath after suffering a coughing fit, she feared for his life. Dragging his chair nearer, she lowered him quickly onto it and looked on with dread. Her concern heightened when, after taking a handkerchief from his pocket, he buried his head into it and coughed and retched until his face turned purple and the handkerchief bore crimson splashes. Noticing, he pushed the handkerchief quickly back inside his pocket. Relief came only when he reached out across his desk and laid a hand on his bible. Charlotte sighed as her father's breathing began to calm and quieten; and Mr Brontë looked to his daughter through weepy, bloodshot eyes.

'But have, have you ever given Nicholls encouragement? Or suspected his intentions?'

'No, never... that he cared for me, I have long since known. But I knew nothing of the depth of his feelings. How could I?' Charlotte said. Then she smiled nervously, if hopefully, 'But Mr Nicholls is a kind man: he is sincere, reliable and honourable. Will you not take time and reconsider?'

'Never!' Mr Brontë snapped, his vitriol returning. 'Nicholls is not good enough for you, Charlotte, and must have your refusal without delay.'

'But, Papa...'

'Papa, nothing. Find another man,' he again raged. 'Find a man who is deserving of you, Charlotte, for you'll not marry Nicholls as long as I've a hole in my backside. I'll not allow it. Not ever!'

Charlotte nipped her lips tight together.

'Never did I think I'd witness the day when you, parson and respected member of the parish, would resort to such vulgarities.'

'That scoundrel drives me to it. Give Nicholls your refusal, and be done.'

'Very well, if that is your wish it will be done,' she snapped. 'But I'll no more stand here and listen to you speak ill of Mr Nicholls... slander his good name,' she said and then stomped toward the door. She yanked it open and turned abruptly back. 'Good night, Papa,' she shouted, and then slammed the door behind her.

'See what he does with his, his...' Mr Brontë shouted after her, and then his tone softened, '...maddens all with his mischief.' He reached across his desk, picked up the magnifying glass and attempted to read a passage from the bible, but his hand trembled and the glass shook and the words were blurred and unreadable. He threw the glass back down, stood up and snatched the lighted candle from his desk and shuffled toward the door carrying it. He opened the door and stepped into the hall, distracted and mumbling. He flinched when Tabby, startled also and her vision fixed upon the stairs, almost walked into him.

'Has everyone gone mad?' The servant cried. 'Charlotte's only this minute flown upstairs ranting, and now you!'

'No one's gone mad, Tabby,' Mr Brontë snapped. 'Some, though, are maddened to distraction by that damnable curate.'

'Mr Brontë!' Tabby shrieked, astounded and glaring. 'Such blasphemous language, and in God's residence! You'll summon a plague to finish us all. The good Lord hears all.'

'Then the good Lord will see that I am right!'

'Right, Mr Brontë?'

'That, that scheming Irish goat, Nicholls, has proposed to my daughter.'

Tabby chuckled. 'And that's put you in a temper!' She said. 'A proposal of marriage! Why a happy occasion should put thunder in your heart and inflame your brain, I'll never know. If Mr Nicholls wishes to marry Charlotte, and she's happy to marry him, where's the harm in that?'

'Where's the harm!' Mr Brontë retorted, glaring. 'Charlotte's all I—'

'If Mr Nicholls loves Charlotte,' Tabby interrupted, 'and she loves him, what reason is there to object? Mr Nicholls is pious, he's upright and he's served you well, Mr Brontë, you know he has.'

'But, but Charlotte's my last surviving child.'

'Aye, and terribly alone without her sisters, and brother – God bless them. She's in need of a companion, someone to share her life… share her bed these cold winter nights.'

'Share her bed!' Mr Brontë repeated, exasperated. 'Better to thwart that Irish fortune-hunting upstart in his speculations before he—'

'Irish fortune-hunting upstart!' Tabby cut in, glaring. 'The same could be said of another ambitious and spirited Irishman not a spit away from where I stand,' she said and chuckled.

Mr Brontë pinched his lips together and glared after Tabby as she hobbled away and disappeared inside the kitchen. Mr Brontë climbed up the stairs, stopping by the alcove and soothing his injured pride in his nightly ritual, winding up the clock.

Demoralized and deprived of sleep, Charlotte sauntered into the dining room the next morning, flashing a furtive glance toward her father, before pulling out a chair. Mr Brontë, spooning porridge into his mouth, stopped the spoon midway and watched while Charlotte sat on the chair opposite; she shuffled the chair under the table and then the spoon continued its route to his mouth.

Seconds later, Tabby hobbled in carrying a bowl of porridge, which she set down on the table in front of Charlotte. The servant, shaking her head, looked first to Mr Brontë, and then to Charlotte.

'What sour faces! You both look like you've slept all night with your noses pushed into the night soil,' she said, nipping her lips together, pausing before continuing. 'If a marriage proposal causes such misery and ill will, thank God I've received none.'

Father and daughter looked to Tabby, but neither spoke. The servant, shaking her head, passed another glance over them both, and then turned and limped from the room, chuckling sardonically. Charlotte picked up the milk jug and poured a small amount onto her porridge. She took a spoon and stirred; she tasted the porridge but, having little appetite for it, released the spoon in the dish and pushed it away, and then turned to her father.

'Did you speak with Mr Nicholls this morning?'

'I did not,' he answered icily. 'How can I when he purposely avoids me?'

'But I thought you might—'

'Might! Might what?' He snapped, and then in the next instant his mood lightened and the right corner of his mouth turned up. 'Nicholls did leave a note, though: a letter of resignation.'

'You'll surely not accept!'

'It's his wish. Who am I to interfere with the plans of another?'

'You interfere with mine.'

Mr Brontë glared. 'Well... Nicholls seeks a position elsewhere.'

'But where!'

'How should I know?'

'Did he not say?'

'He scribbled some half-baked notion of missionary work in—'

'Missionary work!'

'In Australia, I believe.'

'Australia! But that's at the other end of the world!'

Mr Brontë scoffed. 'Nicholls will not go to Australia, Charlotte. His words are those of a vain man thwarted in his speculations.'

'Speculations nothing. Mr Nicholls is heartbroken. He loves me—'

'Love, huh! What does Nicholls know of love?'

'Why should he not know?' Charlotte snapped, and then

sighed and her voice turned tremulous. 'Poor Mr Nicholls…
he suffers terribly for my sake.'

'Nicholls suffers from his own folly.'

Charlotte pushed her chair back noisily along the floor.
The grating noise made Mr Brontë cringe and he brought the
spoon to halt before his lips once again.

'I'll listen to no more,' Charlotte retorted, rising from
her chair and storming away. She turned back. 'I'm glad I'm
going to London in the morning; glad to escape all this, all
this unnecessary nastiness.'

Chapter Eighteen

Unable to sleep, Charlotte was tired and irritable when she boarded the London-bound train in Leeds. The wheels screeching on the iron tracks, the smell of smoke and whale oil and the juddering and rocking all contributed to her discomfort. Added to that, the carriage was stuffy; it was overcrowded and she was wedged between the perspiring bulks of odorous bodies, whose close proximity raised the temperature to an uncomfortable degree: she felt nauseous and was desperate to reach her destination. But for all her distress, the warmth, the motion of the train, or both, had at some point, charmed her senses and induced sleep. When she next became conscious of the world, London was passing by on both sides of the carriage.

Sleep had relaxed her; she felt calm and at peace and by the time the train pulled into Euston Station, Charlotte felt a different person to the one she had left behind in Haworth.

While in London, Charlotte stayed at the family home of her publisher, Mr George Smith, and the next day she walked with him to the company's offices in Cornhill. Allocated a desk in the same room as Mr Smith, she put all disruptive thoughts of home from her mind and quickly set about her task of correcting the proofs of *Villette*. Amending phrases and sentences, correcting spelling errors, checking the grammar, scoring out entire sentences and writing new ones in their place. It was the last opportunity that Charlotte would have of improving her work, before her manuscript was delivered to the printers.

Working in the same office as Mr Smith, though, was not without its problems, as Charlotte soon discovered. The arrangement presented the publisher with an opportunity to appeal to her to alter aspects of her work that he was unhappy with (motivated, no doubt, by the potential for generating greater profit). Confident that he had a better measure of his readers' preferences, Mr Smith appealed to Charlotte to change the ending of *Villette*.

'Please, Currer Bell,' he pleaded for the umpteenth time, peeping playfully around a stack of conveniently positioned manuscripts, alternating an imploring stare with an exaggerated smile.

'It will gain you nothing behaving like a simpleton, Mr Smith. My mind is set,' Charlotte said, glaring back.

'But, Charlotte—'

'Charlotte nothing, Mr Smith, I refuse to amend the ending of *Villette* for no other reason than to satisfy your soppy sentimentality.'

'But, Charlotte, readers all like a happy ending – damn it, they expect it.'

'Readers expect nothing of the kind, Mr Smith.'

'A happy ending leaves the reader feeling satisfied – eager to read more of your novels, Charlotte!'

'From my experience, Mr Smith, readers enjoy experiencing the thrill of the unexpected. And in any case I write true to life; true to the different directions that we humans have forced upon us as we journey through life, and death is a fundamental part of that journey. Death is the concluding act for all living organisms and has been for every creature that has ever lived: it will be the same in a thousand years' time.'

'But it would take little to fashion a happy ending, Charlotte.'

'Paul Emanuel will not live, Mr Smith, he will go down with the ship returning from the West Indies and drown.'

'Charlotte, please... for the sake of Lucy Snowe, if for no other reason.'

'Lucy Snowe is as I am, Mr Smith, bereft. Life is harsh: it is unbelievably cruel. I carry the emotional scars as proof: deep wounds that will not heal, wounds that will torment and torture me for every minute of every hour of every day, and will do so until the day I die, if I live to be a thousand. Were life one long fairy story, I should have a mother, a brother and four sisters, and, as you are aware, Mr Smith, I have none. And pray, where is my knight in shining armour? A strong man riding to my rescue, a kind man who will sweep me up in his arms and carry me through life, bandage my wounds and soothe my pain? *Villette*'s ending reflects real life and life's cruel realities.'

Mr Smith smiled. 'Mr Nicholls may yet be that man, Charlotte – your own true gallant knight!'

'He will not if Papa has his way.'

'But you are a mature, intelligent woman with a mind of your own, with feelings and needs of your own!'

'You know nothing of Papa's obstinacy, Mr Smith.'

The publisher sighed, but then his features brightened all of a sudden.

'But when you write fiction, Charlotte, you hold within your pen the power to be God, to be a good and compassionate God,' He said, his smile widening. 'One that extends life to Paul Emanuel!'

'Stop it, Mr Smith, please... I refuse to create a happy ending solely for the sake of it,' she said, and then resumed her work.

Mr Smith had not abandoned hope though. His eyes remained focussed on Charlotte, and she, conscious of his unrelenting stare, after ignoring him for some minutes, sighed resignedly as she blotted her work.

'Weak-willed men…' she began. 'You are all alike: dewy-eyed romantics. My father is just the same. He, too, pleaded with me to change the ending of *Villette*. He, too, had romantic visions of Professor Paul Emanuel and Lucy Snowe sailing away together – so to speak – under the golden rays of a glorious sunset.'

'There you are, then, Charlotte, male readers – women also, I'm sure – will all feel uplifted with a story that ends happily.' Mr Smith's smile widened. 'Please, Charlotte it would make me happy.'

'Oh, for heaven's sake, Mr Smith—'

'A compromise, then, Charlotte! An ending that at least offers hope for Paul and Lucy!'

'A fairy tale…' Charlotte mocked and then she sat motionless for a while, deep in thought, before sighing and removing her spectacles. 'Very well, Mr Smith, in order to appease your feelings, and to please the readers – and Papa – I'll render the fate of Paul Emanuel open to interpretation. That's my last word. Take it before I change my mind.'

Mr Smith smiled. 'Very well—'

'And do not consider it a victory.'

'Charlotte!' Mr Smith enthused, rubbing his hands together. 'Mother will be delighted.'

'Your mother!'

Mr Smith did appear victorious. He reached out and slid the pile of manuscripts back into their former position on his desk, hiding quickly the self-congratulatory smile that had broken upon his lips.

Charlotte sighed and replaced her spectacles, and then smiled and shook her head and turned over another page. After mouthing the words of a sentence, she picked up her pen and dipped it in the inkwell.

Chapter Nineteen

Charlotte worked tirelessly on her manuscript over the coming days and when she reached the final chapter of the third volume, it was with some regret that, as promised to Mr Smith, she effected the changes to the ending of her story. Leaving the fate of Professor Paul Emanuel on board the ship returning from the West Indies on a stormy sea open to interpretation. Challenging readers to decide for themselves whether Paul Emanuel swam ashore and survived the shipwreck, and if the romance between him and Lucy Snowe resumed and blossomed and resulted in their marriage.

In exalted mood, Charlotte presented the final section of her corrected draft to her publisher.

'And before you ask, Mr Smith, yes, I did keep my promise.'

'God bless you, Charlotte. Your readers will be happy.'

'And your promise to me?'

'Likewise, Charlotte, I shall honour it. Even if I find it an odd request,' he said. 'For the life of me I cannot imagine many people who, when presented with the choice of visiting the many attractions that London has to offer, would choose a tour of Newgate Prison.' Mr Smith looked to her and smiled. 'Research for a future novel?'

The next day, Mr Smith, with little enthusiasm for the adventure himself, escorted Charlotte along Newgate Street toward the imposing prison building. The closer to the institution they became, the tighter she gripped Mr Smith's arm. When they stood before the studded oak door and heard the screams and groans of the inmates, Charlotte shuddered.

'Are you sure you wish to proceed?'

Charlotte smiled and nodded, but her smile disappeared instantly when the prison door flew open and a burly warder, clutching a heavy truncheon, stepped out. His stern stare, his unshaven, greasy face, and his tatty attire gave pause to suspect that he, too, might easily be mistaken for a prisoner.

Eyeing the visitors and scowling, the warder held the door open and beckoned them enter with a cursory nod, and then with a threatening wave of his truncheon and an unintelligible grunt when they were slow to respond. Charlotte's eyes flitted nervously from the warder, to his truncheon, and she fell in behind Mr Smith. Both entered the prison with misgivings.

Charlotte retook Mr Smith's arm and her grip tightened instinctively when the prison door slammed shut behind them. Plunged them into the foul smelling institution, she quickly pulled out a handkerchief and held it over her mouth and nose, while flashing an uncertain glance toward Mr Smith: he grimaced and shrugged.

The prison warder unlocked an iron gate, and with the motion of his truncheon, bid them pass through. Chuckling unnervingly, he slammed the gate behind them, locked it and led them on through the foreboding institution. The presence of stranger's passing through provoked excitable shrieks from the inmates: dirty-faced men and women dressed in rags, and small children caged securely behind iron bars in filthy, cramped enclosures.

'Silence, dogs,' the warder growled and then turned to the visitors. 'This way…'

Grasping hands reached out through the bars, forcing Charlotte and Mr Smith to duck and weave, to twist and turn in order to avoid them. Mr Smith tried his best to keep Charlotte moving along, but she, traumatised and appalled by the abject squalor that she witnessed, dawdled. She halted and let go of Mr Smith's arm when the tiny hand of a frail young girl was extended toward her. Lowering the handkerchief, she took the girl's grimy hand into hers, and smiled.

'What's your name?'

'Anne,' the girl replied nervously, her frightened gaze flitting from Charlotte to the warder.

Charlotte's smile widened. 'My sister was called Anne.'

The scowling warder stormed closer, smashing his truncheon against the iron bars close to the terrified girl; she lurched back. Charlotte was both startled and incensed and her smile disappeared.

'Visitor are not permitted to communicate with the prisoners, ma'am,' he bellowed. The girl attempted to free her hand, but Charlotte clung tight to it.

'She's a child for pity's sake!' Charlotte protested, glaring at the warder towering above her. 'What terrible crime can she possibly be guilty of to deserve—?'

'Move back, wretch,' the warder growled, looking past Charlotte to the girl, striking the iron bars again with his truncheon. The girl struggled to free her hand, but Charlotte continued to hold on.

'Stop! Stop it, please,' Charlotte pleaded.

'It's no use, Charlotte,' Mr Smith said, taking her arm. 'Come—'

'Move along, sir,' the warder bellowed, glaring at Mr Smith. 'And take your lady with you sir. Move! Move!'

'She's not my…' Mr Smith glared back. 'Come, Charlotte.'

'Release the girl, please,' Charlotte begged. 'She's but a child... I'll take her home with me. I'll look after her.'

'She's a criminal, ma'am, and she'll stay where she is. Move!' He roared, raising his truncheon and forming the impression that he might strike her should she fail to comply. Charlotte cowed instinctively and the bond with the girl was broken when the warder began smashing his truncheon against the bars like a man gone mad. The young girl was swallowed up among the mass of protesting, jeering and screaming inmates.

'Come, Charlotte,' Mr Smith urged, himself disturbed by the commotion. 'Let's leave this, this... leave this nightmare behind. Prison is no place for you, or for me,' he said, taking her arm and hurrying her on.

Charlotte, troubled still by the image of the child, turned back; she saw the girl's empty stare, her face pressed up against the cold iron bars, distorting her innocence. Their eyes met briefly, and the girl smiled but in the next instant she was lost amid the jostling, protesting prisoners. Charlotte lifted the handkerchief back up over her mouth as Mr Smith, fending off the inmates' outstretched hands, hurried her toward the exit.

The smirking warder unlocked the gate and opened it, and Charlotte and Mr Smith stepped eagerly through, cringing at the screams and shouts of the inmates and at the warder, who appeared entertained greatly by the prisoners' plight, standing grinning, bellowing back at them, baiting the hapless inmates like it was some kind of game.

Writer and publisher, relieved and breathing easier, stepped gratefully from the prison and into the sanitized air of the busy London street. Thankful for the sun's timely appearance, as it slid silently from behind an iridescent orange cloud, as if to remind them of the simple pleasures that prison denies the wrongdoers of this world. They stood a moment and basked in the sun's life-enhancing balm, inhaling the nectar of freedom with the zest of persons released after a lifetime's incarceration.

'Well, Charlotte,' Mr Smith said. 'If that's not grist to feed your imagination, I don't know what is!'

'I cannot believe that such places exist still, Mr Smith. Those poor people crammed into such a small space. Forced to suffer appalling degradation and cruelty at the hands of brutes. Denied respect and compassion – values that you and I take for granted.'

'Yes, yes, Charlotte, but don't forget they are in prison for a reason. They are criminals, judged to have committed crimes, or they would not be there.'

'Whatever their crimes, any decent citizen would surely recoil being witness to the appalling conditions that fellow humans are forced to suffer. Those despairing faces – and that poor child.'

'Yes, yes, and I'm sure the images will haunt and torment our consciences for some time to come, Charlotte,' Mr Smith said, and then he forced a smile. 'It'll perhaps help keep us on the path of righteousness!'

'But that poor young girl…' Charlotte said, distractedly. 'Her plight demands pause for thought surely. If only that we may consider how fortunate you and I are, Mr Smith. For in different circumstances it might have been me behind those bars… one of my sisters, or more likely my poor, dear brother, Branwell. Evil influences worked their worst on him and steered him into ill ways.'

'Indeed, we should be thankful, Charlotte—'

'Prison, though, cannot be right for that poor girl, for a child so young and fragile. What, I wonder, was her crime?'

Mr Smith grimaced, 'I believe she murdered her illegitimate child.'

'She's but a child herself,' Charlotte protested, her sense of injustice heightening. She faced Mr Smith and her tone hardened. 'And what of the child's father?'

'I, I believe he had no hand in the child's death.'

'No, but he was present at the child's conception, and then in all likelihood he abandoned the poor, pregnant girl; left her to her fate, to suffer alone with no thought at all for her welfare. And I'll wager anything that he remains free, free to seek out other gullible young girls, satisfy his carnal urges and then disappear. How can it be right that he is spared justice and punishment?'

'Men will, well...' Mr Smith sighed, somewhat apologetically. 'Well, I cannot deny, judgement, it seems, falls favourably with men. The world is unjust, Charlotte. It is cruel and unforgiving but where one is helpless to right a wrong, it's better to look away. Put the misery of others from your mind before it eats into your soul and drags you into its bile.'

Charlotte shook her head. 'Sometimes when I sit alone on dreary winter nights with only my thoughts, images of happier days come effortlessly to my mind. Those days are gone now, I know, but I relish every precious memory, and that I was fortunate enough to share simple, carefree pleasures with people I loved and cared for. I think of dear Mama, my brother and four sisters, and wonder if they are not better off out of it. They are at rest in a peaceful place where the evils of this world cannot touch them anymore.'

Mr Smith sighed. 'Judgement day will come to us all, Charlotte.'

'Indeed it will, Mr Smith, when, after a lifetime of suffering, we are no more. Swept nonchalantly aside and gone, like a passing cloud.'

'Poor, Charlotte! When you are in Manchester, Elizabeth Gaskell will perhaps restore your spirits, help re-establish your faith in human nature. Come,' Mr Smith urged, drawing her to his side and taking her arm. 'Mother will be anxious if we are late back for dinner – anxious or angry.'

'Angry perhaps,' Charlotte said and laughed.

Mr Smith smiled and then, encouraged by him, they picked up their pace as they threaded their way through the bustling hoards on London's busy streets, streets alive with people whose vibrant voices sang above the clatter of the horses' hooves and the sound of carriage wheels turning over the gravel.

Chapter Twenty

Liberated from the disciplines and demands of work and removed from the hectic pace of London life, Charlotte felt able to relax. At the Manchester home of Mrs Gaskell, she erased from her mind all that had vexed her in London, putting aside the hurtful episode that had erupted with Mr Nicholls' proposal. Gone were the headaches, the nausea and the sleepless nights. Charlotte's mood lightened, her spirits rose. She felt healthier and stronger than in weeks, and, in the company of the Gaskell's four girls, she, too, felt younger. Immersing herself willingly into the pleasing hub of family life. She took a keen interest in the eldest girls' needlework skills, helping Marianne and Margaret hone their work. She joined in with their games, brushed and plaited their hair and when bedtime approached, she sat them around in a semi-circle on the rug and recited stories to them of Haworth, of its characters amid the wild and windswept moorland, as they sipped their nighttime drink of warm milk.

Secure within Mrs Gaskell's commodious and magnificent home, Charlotte was able to enjoy that which had ordinarily evaded her most: a peaceful night's sleep. Opulent dreams chased away troubling nightmares; and she dreamed that she was a princess cocooned within the safe space of a luxurious palace, a dazzling white palace, warmed by the sun and fragranced with the intoxicating scents of exotic flowers. On awakening she discovered that she indeed lay in a similar pleasing environment; a fabulous room in her host's fine house, suffused with the scent of newly-picked flowers and, like in her dream, bathed in the early morning sunshine.

She rose early and breakfasted with Mrs Gaskell on toast and marmalade and coffee; it was a rushed affair, since both were keen to take advantage and walk out under the warm sunshine. They put on their bonnets and coats and stepped out into the brilliant spring morning and arm in arm they strolled cheerfully across the dew-spangled grass. Purging their lungs in the fresh morning air, conversing and smiling, admiring the shrubbery as they advanced across the clipped lawn. Then Mrs Gaskell drew Charlotte to a sudden halt.

'Look, Charlotte…' she said, resting a plump bud on an upturned palm. 'Beautiful magnolia buds, swelling already with the warming days.' She let go of it and with a sweep of an arm, drew Charlotte's eyes upward. 'Scores of them, eager to burst into life and display their beauty the moment they are awakened by the warm spring sunshine.'

'That I had similar prospects to look to,' Charlotte said somewhat glumly.

'But life cannot surely be all emptiness and sadness?'

'Truly, it is, Lily. The loss of my sisters is felt much keener now that my novel is finished. My days are largely unoccupied; they are unbearable and stretch endlessly ahead, and the nights, well…'

'You need something apart from writing, Charlotte. An interest to focus upon and absorb your energies, an occupation that will engage your mind and chase away indulgent thought.'

'Others say the same, but what?'

'Mine, as you are aware, when I'm not writing revolves

around my family; my four girls and William promote untold joy. They make for a happy and fulfilled life – keep my mind occupied at all times and steer me from idle thought.'

'But a similar prospect, for me is indeed remote.'

'Perhaps it is, but had you a man to share your life with, well... that would be a start.'

'Finding the right man is not easy,' Charlotte said, and then scoffed. 'But finding a man who is acceptable to Papa is virtually impossible.'

'Is there really no hope then of resurrecting your friendship with Mr Nicholls?' Mrs Gaskell asked, taking Charlotte's arm and leading her on.

'That chapter is closed for good,' she said and sighed. 'Mr Nicholls has resigned from Papa's church and is to move away.'

'By your tone, I suspect you hold some affection for the love-struck curate?'

'As a friend, well, yes, always,' Charlotte said and paused. 'But then again, when Mr Nicholls proposed, well... it came as a complete surprise, and I cannot deny it awoke feelings within me I never knew existed. I was flattered, excited... now I am confused and in all honesty know not what my true feelings are. Perhaps I was desperate for a man to love me!'

'Disparage not yourself, Charlotte! A proposal, even if it comes from a man for whom you previously felt little or nothing at all, it excites one's blood all the same.'

'Indeed... and I cannot deny Mr Nicholls' proposal put my heart in a flutter.'

'And you did, after all, adopt 'Bell' for your nom de plume!'

'Oh, but the name Bell was taken at Emily's insistence for anonymity when, with she and Anne and me, we published our small volume of poetry together.'

Mrs Gaskell smiled and with a gentle gesture encouraged Charlotte to walk on some more. They strolled on together in silence for a while, luxuriating under the warm sun and listening to the chorus of the awakening world. Stopping periodically in order that they might admire the greening foliage at close proximity, or drool over the soft warm colours of the daffodils and primroses. Mrs Gaskell turned to Charlotte, smiling encouragingly. 'Unless you feel nothing at all for Mr Nicholls, Charlotte, you really ought to reconsider his offer,' she said. 'For, from what you have told me he seems a kind and caring man, and his proposal appears genuine. Mr Nicholls, I'm sure, would make a splendid husband.'

Charlotte shrugged. 'It's done with him, Lily. Mr Nicholls and I no longer speak. In fact I take every opportunity of avoiding him. For if by chance we meet, he troubles me with doleful looks, yet...' she said and paused, halted and drew Mrs Gaskell to a stop also. 'I wish him no ill, and nor do I dislike him. For, when someone declares a fondness for me, I cannot help but like them. And ever since the night Mr Nicholls' proposed, I've been unable to banish his image from my head. Poor man, he stood before me trembling like a leaf on a tree in a breeze... struggling terribly with hard-wrought words.'

'Like the magnolia buds, Charlotte, responding to the warming spring days, unfurling their beauty and wooing the bees, your heart, too, has been tempted. Awakened by overtures of love, and love often germinates from improbable beginnings, gathering momentum and growing, blossoming into something rather more wonderful and beautiful.' She halted, bent down and plucked a weed from the soil and tossed it onto the compost heap. 'If hope remains, Charlotte, and if you feel that a union with Mr Nicholls might bring happiness back into your life, do not squander the opportunity. Weed out doubt and see what remains.'

'But you know I could not marry without Papa's blessing.'

'Charlotte, you'll be forty in a few years' time! You do not need your father's permission to marry. And in any case he can be brought round later?'

'I'm not sure that he can, Lily.'

'But your father would surely not stand in the way of your happiness! You are his last surviving child, and from the things you say, his affection for you is obvious. Charlotte, your father loves you.'

'I wonder at times if he does, for you should have seen him on the night Mr Nicholls proposed. Papa worked himself into an explosive state; his face was on fire, and the veins at his temple stood proud and looked like they would burst – perhaps they would had I not backed down and agreed to his wishes.'

Mrs Gaskell, shaking her head, stroked Charlotte's arm.

'Poor, Charlotte! Men are predisposed to display their tyrannical side in order to get their way.' She said and then paused. 'But tell me, how did Mr Nicholls accept your refusal?'

'I know not how, Lily. I wrote him a note. Martha delivered it the next day.'

'Oh, Charlotte!'

'I cannot imagine it being taken easily, poor man. He trembled at my feet on the night he proposed.'

Mrs Gaskell chuckled. 'And we women are labelled the weaker sex!'

'Oh, but you would not mock, Lily. Mr Nicholls' world is now filled with gloom. Papa makes light of it – it amuses him no end – but it saddens me greatly.'

'Then affection does exist!'

'I cannot tell what, Lily, but I confess my heart has been in turmoil ever since the night Mr Nicholls' proposed.'

'Instinct tells me that your feelings run deeper than you'll admit to, Charlotte,' Mrs Gaskell said, looking intently at her. 'Re-establish your friendship with Mr Nicholls... keep him in sight until you are sure.'

'He speaks now of emigrating to Australia.'

'Australia!' Mrs Gaskell exclaimed, and then chuckled. 'A typical reaction when love is thwarted. Run away... escape from the heartbreak, the emotional turmoil and begin again in an exotic land,' she said and smiled. 'It's right that your father should be protective, Charlotte, but do not let an opportunity pass by in order to appease his prejudices and jealousies.'

'Jealousies!'

'Your father is afraid of losing you – to another man.'

'But—'

'Keep Arthur Bell Nicholls interested, Charlotte... do not lose sight of him.'

Leaving Mrs Gaskell's home was always a wrench, and Charlotte wished that she could stay longer – the four girls almost changed her mind – but thoughts of her father began to unsettle her. They had parted on less than cordial terms; his blood was up and she had been desperate to escape from the grip of his tyranny. But he was her father, and she knew that, despite everything that had happened and everything that had been said, he would be anxious until she was safely back home.

'When you visit next, you'll perhaps bring a husband?' Mrs Gaskell said, as she and Charlotte walked toward the awaiting carriage.

'It's unlikely to be Mr Nicholls.'

'Restore your friendship with him, Charlotte, and see what develops. For if Mr Nicholls is able to bring only a modicum of happiness back into your life, well...'

The coachman, standing holding the carriage door open, shuffled his feet on the gravel and glanced impatiently toward them. His imploring stare seemed well practiced. Charlotte smiled, she embraced and kissed Mrs Gaskell, and then climbed on board the coach. The driver closed the door and Mrs Gaskell stepped up to the carriage.

'If you feel that Mr Nicholls might be right for you, Charlotte, do not be deterred by your father's opposition and stubbornness. Renew your friendship with Mr Nicholls before he disappears from your life forever.'

The coachman climbed on board and shuffled into position; he picked up his whip, cracked it over the horses' backs and shouted to the animals to walk on. Mrs Gaskell stood back and, above the sound of the coachman's voice, the clatter of horses' hooves and the crunch of gravel, the two writers called to each other and waved until each was lost to the other.

Chapter Twenty-One

Tabby, smiling distractedly and lost to thoughts of her own, swept the leaves and dust up on the floor in hall. She began teasing them into a neat pile with the broom, when a knock on the door startled her. Flossy raced out from the dining room, barking and scattering the leaves back across the floor.

'Blasted animal,' shrieked Tabby, raising the brush. 'I'll…' The knock was repeated. 'Enter!'

Flossy, unable to distinguish between a reprimand and a show of affection, sidled up to Tabby, panting and wagging his tail. The servant, frowning and shaking her head, lowered the brush, and then quickly straightened her attire when the door was pushed open.

'Mr Nicholls! Well, don't stand loitering on the doorstep! Come on in, come.'

'Thank you, Tabby,' he cut in. 'But I'll not stay,' he said firmly, shifting uncomfortably, shuffling reluctantly into the hall. He smiled when Flossy jumped up at his side, and he stroked and patted the excitable animal.

'Well, shut the door.'

He pushed it to, but did not latch it. 'I called only to inform you that I'll be leaving.'

'You've been invisible for days and everyone thought you'd gone already! And poor, neglected Flossy, he's fair missed his walks on the moors, haven't you, poor thing?' Tabby said, looking down upon the dog. She turned to Mr

Nicholls, smiling warmly. 'Kettle's only this minute boiled, I'll make you a mug of beef tea.'

'Thank you, Tabby, but no… I came only to let you know I'll be leaving the parish at the end of the month.'

'But that's next week,' Tabby cried, frowning and shaking her head. 'Many'll be sorry to see you go.'

'Others will be equally glad that I am gone,' Mr Nicholls said bitterly, as his eyes flitted about. His tone softened and then he smiled. 'Is, is Miss Brontë back from Manchester yet?'

'No.' Tabby said curtly. 'She might be back today, she might be back tomorrow, she might be back next week.' She resumed her work, sweeping the leaves and dust back into a pile.

Mr Nicholls stood observing her for some seconds.

'Perhaps I'm never to see Charlotte again,' he bemoaned. 'Destiny…'

Tabby halted and glared at him. 'Destiny my fanny aunt!' She snapped, resting on the brush shaft, breathing labouredly – from irritation rather than from the effort expended sweeping the floor. 'You won't see Charlotte, will you, if you're set on running away like a flea-bitten chicken?' Her elevated tone set Flossy off barking. 'Quiet, you daft hound!' she shouted, lifting the brush and feigning to strike the animal again.

'Running away!' Mr Nicholls repeated, exasperated. 'But I—'

'Aye, running away,' Tabby shouted, and then she turned the brush on him. 'Aye, go on, run, you spineless shyster, and take that noisy blasted animal with you.'

Mr Nicholls crouched. 'But, but…'

Tabby calmed her temper and lowered the brush while glaring still. 'Men from these parts are as tough as the rocks on the moor and I thought you Irishmen were of a similar breed, but it seems I was wrong.'

Mr Nicholls, affronted, glared back. 'Say what you will, Tabby, but I'll not come between a father and his daughter,' he said, turning abruptly, pulling open the door and stepping outside.

'You give in too easily, if you ask me,' Tabby shouted after him. 'Charlotte's not as immovable as her father,' she said, taking a hand brush and shovel. She bent down and swept the dirt and leaves onto the shovel, and then carried it toward the open door. 'Win her heart and she'll fight; Charlotte will fight where you will not – dare not.'

After descending the steps, he turned back and glared but he remained tight-lipped and watched as Tabby, tottering in the doorway holding the shovel, cast the dust and leaves from it. The wind blew it back over her; she coughed and spat and then shot a scornful glance toward the departing curate.

'Well, you now know my thoughts,' she shouted.

'Farewell, Tabby,' Mr Nicholls called back without turning, striding away along the garden path. A smile, though, manifested its presence on his lips; it widened with each retreating step.

Flossy made a dash for the exit, but he was not quick enough. Tabby grabbed hold of his collar and dragged the thwarted animal back inside, and then shut the door. Released, the dog sauntered forlornly toward the kitchen; and Tabby, shaking her head and watching, started when the study door flew open.

'What did Nicholls want?' Mr Brontë demanded. Tabby, her breath stolen and clutching her chest was slow to respond, and he continued. 'Conniving scoundrel… you're not to let him into my home ever again.'

'Your obstinacy might have crushed Charlotte's hopes – for now,' Tabby began. 'But if her heart's set on Mr Nicholls, be assured your stubbornness will count for nothing. It'll make her more determined. Charlotte's hewn from the same stern stuff as her father, and she's as strong-willed – and pig-headed.'

Mr Brontë's lips tightened and he glared hard at the servant, but then his tone softened.

'But, but all I've ever wanted is what's best for my daughter,' he said.

Tabby shook her head.

Tabby was later proved right: Charlotte, having returned from Manchester while Mr Nicholls remained in the parish, was determined to be at the church and hear his farewell sermon. Arriving late, she crept into the church and settled into the pews at the rear. Mr Nicholls, having already begun his sermon, noticed; his voice faltered and he halted. Heads turned to see upon whom the curate's eyes were trained. Mr Nicholls, discomfited, cleared his throat and in a tremulous voice resumed, stuttering and stopping and restarting, and then when words failed him completely, he pulled out a handkerchief, blew his nose and dabbed his eyes. After taking several deep breaths, he summoned the strength to continue and he struggled on to the end. It was a dismal performance, though, and many in attendance left the church bemused and disappointed.

The following morning when Charlotte joined her father at the breakfast table, he looked scornfully to her. Then a wry smile began to lift the right corner of his lip; he appeared impatient to speak, but he waited until Charlotte was seated.

'You mentioned nothing to me last night of Nicholls' shameful performance in the pulpit.'

'Why should I?' Charlotte retaliated. 'Mr Nicholls has suffered enough humiliation?'

'Humiliation nothing… bah, unmanly driveller displaying his emotions for all to witness – and in a place of worship.'

'You are un-Christian, unforgiving and unnecessarily harsh.'

'Harsh! Nonsense!'

'What then of your Christian values of showing compassion?'

'Nicholls deserves none,' Mr Brontë snapped. 'And the sooner the Judas is gone from this parish the better for everyone.'

'Don't pretend that you speak for me, or for anyone else for that matter, for you do not,' Charlotte snapped, pushing her chair noisily back along the floor, rising and then storming away. Mr Brontë, watching, jumped when she slammed the door after exiting. Shaking his head, he sighed but turned back to the porridge and scraped every last oat from the bowl.

Mr Nicholls was left with one final task before taking leave of the parish: paperwork pertinent to his position at the church required returning to his employer. On the said evening, Charlotte, aware of his presence in her father's study, stood hidden from view on the landing and attempted to listen in on the men's conversation. Hoping, praying perhaps, that her father might change his mind and grant permission for their friendship to resume. It was a forlorn hope though.

Parish business concluded and Mr Nicholls emerged from the study. Appearing in no hurry to leave, his eyes flitted anxiously about; and he put on his coat, hat and scarf, as slowly as was possible while looking in turn toward the dining room, to the stairs and to the kitchen, sighing and sniffing. Once fully attired, and having no further reason to dawdle, he grimaced and then sauntered forlornly toward the exit, turning back several times, before opening the door and stepping outside.

Charlotte, from her concealed position on the landing, looked down and watched as the man that might have been her husband, walked out of her life. When the parsonage door slammed shut she ran into her room and up to the window, from where she looked out in the hope of capturing one last glimpse of Mr Nicholls.

She watched and waited, but the curate failed to appear. Though the night was pitch black, it seemed impossible that he could have slipped away unnoticed. Puzzled and frowning, Charlotte pressed her face close to the glass panes and looked in every direction, but Mr Nicholls, it seemed, had mysteriously disappeared.

Chapter Twenty-Two

Charlotte meandered away from the window, puzzled and ponderous. But then her eyes widened and she halted abruptly, stepped back to the window and listened upon hearing what sounded like the soft pulsating echo of someone sobbing. Frowning, she looked about once again, but still she could see no one, and then, while deep in thought, she paused a moment before hurrying from her room. She crept down the stairs, tiptoed across the hall toward the door, opened it and looked out; and there, leaning against the house wall, resting his head on his forearms stood the distressed curate.

'Mr Nicholls, what—'

He looked sharply to her. 'Miss Brontë, I, I…' he stuttered, sniffing and dragging a sleeve across his face. 'I thought I was never to see you again,' he blurted, and then thrust a hand instinctively toward her. 'Walk with me please, just a little—'

'I cannot… will not—'

'Then say something… anything, even if it offers only the tiniest crumb of hope, for the thought of losing you is more than I can bear.'

'Mr Nicholls!'

'I cared for you, Miss Brontë,' he blurted. 'From the moment I first set eyes on you, I cared—'

'Mr Nicholls.'

'I see the day clearly still… you were in the garden reading to your sisters, Emily and Anne. And though they were beautiful, too, it was you, Miss Brontë, you that caught my eye. You were the one that set my heart beating like never before.'

'I'll listen to no more, Mr Nicholls. I must go.'

'No! Wait, please!' He pleaded, reaching out and snatching hold of her arm.

'Let go of my arm,' she snapped, attempting to unfold his fingers. 'Release me at once, Mr Nicholls, or I shall call for Papa.'

'Then you are happy to see me leave, also?' He said, and then reluctantly let go of her arm.

'Yes, no! Oh, I do not know,' Charlotte said and sighed. 'Please do not press for answers you know I cannot give. But I am saddened if you feel you must leave the parish because of me, and I'm truly sorry if I've made you unhappy.'

'I am more than unhappy, I—'

'I must go, Mr Nicholls,' she said and then attempted to close the door, but his foot prevented her. Mr Nicholls' stepped closer and thrust his face close to hers.

'Kiss me, Miss Brontë, grant me just one kiss.'

'Mr Nicholls!'

He reached out and rested a hand gently upon Charlotte's arm. She flinched, but did not struggle or fight him off, and he, taking encouragement from the absence of further resistance, lifted her hand up to his lips and kissed her fingers – a snatched but intense kiss – and she allowed her hand to remain enclosed within his for some seconds more, before snatching it away.

'I must go, Mr Nicholls,' she said. 'I came only to wish you well in your future employment.'

'Tell me that hope exists... that something may yet be done. For I love you, Miss Brontë, really and truly.'

Charlotte gasped.

'Goodbye, Mr Nicholls,' she blurted, and then closed the door.

Her entire body turned instantly tremulous and, breathing heavily, she leant against the door while staring straight ahead through eyes widening with disbelief, with wonderment. Her heart thumped hard inside her breast; and she fingered her face and then put the hand to her lips that Mr Nicholls had kissed. Distracted, she meandered away from the door, flinching and making a sudden dash for the stairs when the study door flew open.

'Has Nicholls gone?' Mr Brontë demanded.

Charlotte, having climbed up several steps, turned round.

'He has.'

'The scoundrel... coming here, distressing everyone.'

'He distresses only you,' Charlotte snapped. 'You are determined to make out that Mr Nicholls is a bad man, when you know very well he is not. He has served you, your church faithfully over many years, and all of a sudden he is a pariah, cast out into the wilderness for what? For falling in love!'

'Love... huh! I thought well enough of Nicholls once, until he came seducing with his Gaelic charm... seeking to elevate his position in attaching to you.'

'He loves me, Papa.'

'Nicholls cares nothing for you, Charlotte. Fame and fortune is all that scoundrel aspires to.'

'To say so is an insult to me. You despise Mr Nicholls for no other reason than out of spite. Your wish is to keep me here always... shackled to your whims until the day you die.

What then of my future?' Charlotte retorted, and then she breathed a conciliatory sigh. 'Oh, Papa, why must we…'

'You are famous writer, Charlotte. Better men will come along…' He said, and he, too, sighed. 'We were happy once…'

'Yes, we were happy, very happy, but Emily, Anne and Branwell were alive then. Now that they are gone my life is desolate. It will remain so if you have your way. You care nothing for my pain, for my heartache, for my future. Good night,' she shouted, and then charged up the remaining stairs, clutching her head. She ran into her room and slammed the door, threw herself down on her bed and then burst into tears.

Mr Brontë, downcast and shuffling uneasily about in the hall near the stairs, could hear his daughter sobbing. Unable to endure her distress and, bearing a pained expression, he hurried toward his study and stepped inside, closing the door on his daughter's heartbreak. He slumped down into his chair, reached out and dragged the lighted candle closer, picked up the magnifying glass, flicked over several pages of the bible and read aloud the words of the psalms. '"Hear my prayer, O Lord, Give ear to my supplications! In your faithfulness answer me…"'

Chapter Twenty-Three

From a friendship that had seemed doomed and done, signs of reconciliation were afoot. Mr Nicholls, unwilling to give up on Charlotte, wrote to her; he wrote on several occasions but received no reply. Determination, though, and perhaps with the sentiment of Tabby's words in his ears, he persevered, and Charlotte, heartened by his persistence and by the sincerity conveyed in his letters, succumbed and finally wrote back. Mr Nicholls was in ecstasies and could hardly believe his good fortune.

Over the coming weeks and months, correspondence flowed regularly between the two lovers. It was at about the same time that Martha appeared to have developed an unusual fascination for the postman. Whenever his tuneless whistle was heard, or if the young servant saw him approaching, she abandoned whatever task she was involved with and ran along the garden path to meet him. Returning to the parsonage with a nonchalant air, dropping off mail addressed to Mr Brontë in the hall, and then her demeanour changed abruptly and she charged about like she was possessed; and Martha was possessed. Running from room to room in an excitable state until locating the whereabouts of Charlotte, upon whom she unburdened herself of the letters concealed about her person.

On days when the postman failed to call, or if he carried no letters for Charlotte addressed in a particular style of handwriting, the young servant mooched about with a despondent air – a mood that afflicted Charlotte also. Martha knew not why she was sad, other than that Charlotte was sad, and she possessed no knowledge of the identity of author of the letters, and knew not why Charlotte had insisted the letters be kept secret from her father. The young servant, though, was not without guile, and one morning, after several days had passed when no letters were delivered to Charlotte, Martha noted her employer's jubilation after being handed such a letter.

'Are the letters from Mr Nicholls?' Martha chanced to ask.

'Shh, Martha!' Charlotte bid her, looking anxiously about. 'You've not said anything about the letters to Papa, have you?'

'No, Miss,' Martha said, slighted by the suggestion that she might betray her confidence.

After discovering the sender of the letters, Martha acquired an increased sense of importance and appeared thrilled at being a trusted participant in the clandestine operation. The opposite, though, was the case for Charlotte; she became increasingly uncomfortable with the secrecy. Mr Nicholls' letters arrived weekly, sometimes twice a week, and it seemed only a matter of time before her father found out. Charlotte was desperate to win him over and decided that the time was right to appeal to him again, hopeful that if her father could be made aware of Mr Nicholls' sincerity, and of her own burgeoning feelings toward his curate, he would surely deny her no longer.

Stepping tentatively toward his study, Charlotte knocked on the door, opened it and stepped inside.

'Charlotte…' he uttered, shuffling round in his chair, gripping the magnifying glass he had been using to help him read.

'Papa, it pains me to keep secrets from you,' she blurted. 'But Mr Nicholls and me —'

'Nicholls!' He cut in angrily, slamming the magnifying glass down on his desk and jumping up out of his chair. 'Will I never hear the last of him? I knew it… knew the scheming toad was up to something behind my back.'

'I'm sorry if it grieves you, Papa, but—'

'How many times must I tell you, Charlotte? That, that Irish goat is not good enough for you? It would be a degradation for you, a famous writer, to marry a low-bred Irish upstart.'

'Upstart, nothing, Papa, Arthur loves me—'

'End all correspondence with Nicholls, Charlotte, and find a man who is deserving of you. Find a man upon whose arm you can be proud to walk through the streets on.'

'Who, then? Tell me who, Papa?'

'I, I…'

'Tell me!' she snapped. 'Who would you have me choose for a husband? Who would you have for your son-in-law?'

'Mr Tay–'

'And don't mention Mr Taylor,' Charlotte snapped. 'You know how I detest him and cannot stand the little man near me for more than one second.'

'But, I—'

'Come, Papa, who?' she demanded, pausing and glaring, looking askance to him. Her father shrugged and shook his head and, after failing to offer an alternative, Charlotte continued. 'The butcher, the baker the night-soil collector. Tell me?' She screamed. 'Mr Rochester! Mr Heathcliff!'

'Silence your insolence…' he raged, and then sighed. 'But, but Mr Taylor is a fine man—'

'Speak no more to me of Mr Taylor,' Charlotte implored.

'Why must you think I should marry him when you know I do not love him?'

'Love, huh!' Mr Brontë uttered. 'Securing your future is more important. But, but you say nothing of your love for Nicholls!'

'His letters have softened my heart, and were I given the chance to know him better, yes, I believe I could love him – unreservedly.'

Mr Brontë sighed and turned. He slumped back down in his chair, picked up the magnifying glass and drew his bible closer.

'Then why try my patience if your mind is already made up?' He said, lowering his head over the bible.

'Arthur and I had hoped to be able to conduct our friendship with your approval.'

'Arthur, is it, indeed…' He scoffed, raising his head and looking to her. 'I am not blind, Charlotte, and have known for weeks that you and Nicholls have been exchanging letters – huh, soppy love letters,' he said, lowering his head. 'Leave me, Charlotte… go and help the servants make our home respectable. It won't do to have the place looking like a pigsty when Mrs Gaskell arrives tomorrow.'

Hard work proved the best therapy. Physical work assisting Tabby and Martha to re-position the furniture, clean the windows and polish the furniture, helped Charlotte take her mind off events and discharge her anger and frustration. The servants were both happy; they enjoyed working with Charlotte and had done so on many occasions before. Martha was especially pleased; being supervised by Charlotte, she felt, would free her from Tabby's tyranny – or so she had hoped.

'More effort, child,' the elderly servant barked, observing Martha wafting the duster lazily over the furniture.

Charlotte, watching and listening, smiled. 'Come, Martha…' she said. 'Help me move these chairs back where they were.'

Tabby scowled and shook her head. 'You shift them here and you shift them there, and then move them back to where they stood in the first place. Leave them be, can't you? You'll not be satisfied until I fall over them and injure my good leg.'

Charlotte smiled. 'Refreshments, Tabby, if you please. Prepare refreshments and then carry them through into the dining room.'

Tabby smiled, sighed and smacked her lips together, which seemed to suggest that she, too, was parched and ready for a drink, and she willingly carried out Charlotte's request, hobbling hurriedly from the dining room.

With Tabby absent, Martha worked with renewed enthusiasm, and when the furniture had been repositioned, Charlotte summoned her to help polish the sideboard, the table and the chairs and soon every spindle shone like new.

'Flowers, Martha, we must procure flowers… Mrs Gaskell's home is scented throughout with the perfume of fresh flowers!'

'I'll see what I can find in the neighbouring gardens.'

'Martha!'

Tabby returned with refreshments, and Charlotte, satisfied that nothing more could be done, invited the two servants to sit with her by the fire. Exhausted but happy, the ladies relaxed in the comfort of the lavender-scented room and enjoyed coffee and biscuits amid cordial conversation.

Chapter Twenty-Four

Horses' hooves and the sound of carriage wheels turning on the cobblestones in the lane signalled the arrival of Mrs Elizabeth Gaskell. Martha, as usual, heard them first and she charged excitedly from room to room, calling to everyone that Charlotte's friend had arrived. Flossy chased after her, barking crazily, and Tabby, immune normally to emotional extremes seemed not to know if she was coming or going. Trying her best to keep pace with Martha, the elderly servant's lips were stretched wider than many thought possible, and Charlotte, breathless herself after hurrying down the stairs, shuffled nervously in the hall, fidgeting with her attire.

Martha opened the parsonage door and hurried outside; she jumped down the steps and ran along the garden path. Flossy chased after her, barking.

'Mrs Gaskell!' The young servant called out, as she approached the garden gate. She opened the gate and stepped eagerly onto the lane. 'We've waited an age and thought you'd changed your mind.'

Mrs Gaskell turned and smiled. 'Well, it's such a long way, and all those steep hills, but I am here now. You must be Martha?' She said, shaking the young servant's hand, and then she looked up and over Martha's head. 'And that's the famous parsonage? The place where so many wonderful stories have been conceived and written.'

The coachman unloaded the suitcases, and Martha, grimacing, picked them up.

'Are they full of books, Miss?'

Mrs Gaskell smiled and shook her head, and her smile widened when Charlotte emerged, descending the steps and waving fervently. The visiting writer reciprocated; she settled her fare quickly and then followed Martha and the gambolling, barking dog.

Charlotte and Mrs Gaskell met along the garden path where they embraced and kissed, and then, conversing animatedly, they strolled together toward the parsonage, watching Martha straining every sinew as struggled up the steps with the heavy suitcases. Flossy impeded the servant's ascent and she stumbled.

'Careful, Martha!' Charlotte called out.

Martha gritted her teeth and continued to the top of the steps and shuffled inside with the suitcases. She set them down on the floor in the hall and stood by them, looking to Charlotte and Mrs Gaskell when they entered.

Mrs Gaskell turned back and looked out over the landscape, inhaling deeply.

'The air blowing from the hills smells clean and sweet,' she said. 'And what wonderful views.'

'We look upon them every day, Lily; to us I'm afraid they seem rather ordinary,' Charlotte said, and then closed the door.

'Well...' Mrs Gaskell said, smiling and looking about. 'What a pleasure– '

'I trust your journey was not too tiring, Lily?'

'Dear me, Charlotte, riding up and down the steep hills is enough to leave one breathless. And those poor horses... they must be desperate for a rest and a drink of water. I trust they are well cared for?'

'Of course they are, Lily. The horses provide their owners with a living. They cannot afford to neglect them.'

Mrs Gaskell loosened the ribbons on her bonnet and removed it, and when she had taken off her coat, Martha darted forward, took the garments from her and hung them on the coat stand.

The study door opened.

'Mrs Gaskell…' Mr Brontë enthused, shuffling into the hall, beaming and extending a hand. 'The famous writer of *Mary Barton*. What a privilege.'

'The privilege is mine, Mr Brontë,' Mrs Gaskell said, shaking his hand. 'It's most gracious of you to accept me into your home.'

'You are welcome,' Mr Brontë said. 'Our home is a modest one, Mrs Gaskell, but I hope it will be acceptable to you.'

'If your home pleases you, Mr Brontë, it will please me also,' she said. 'But please, friends all call me Lily.'

Tabby, determined not to miss out when eminent people visited the parsonage, hobbled out from the kitchen, wiping her hands on her pinafore.

'Mrs Gaskell,' she said, offering her hand.

'Tabby…' The visitor returned, accepting the servant's hand and shaking. 'How delightful… Charlotte is full of praise for your cooking. Indeed, I can hardly wait to sample it. The thought excites my taste buds already.

'It's but simple country fare,' Tabby said.

'Delicious, all the same,' Charlotte added.

'If your biscuits stand as an example – my children loved those that Charlotte brought when she last visited, as indeed did I – then I'll not be disappointed, I'm sure.'

Charlotte gesticulated. 'Come, Lily, I'll show you to your room.'

That was the cue for Martha. She bent down, picked up the suitcases and made for the stairs, stumbling and faltering as she ascended them.

'Careful, Martha, careful!' Charlotte and Mrs Gaskell called out together, turning to each other and laughing.

Chapter Twenty-Five

With a mind of making life easier, and at every opportunity, Tabby, after seeing Charlotte and Mrs Gaskell putting on their coats in the hall, bemoaned the scarcity of dripping. Charlotte volunteered to call at the butchers and purchase a quantity. In her next breath the servant complained she was almost out of bread and needed flour and yeast, and Martha was busy disinfecting the closet. Charlotte volunteered again, even though a visit to the stationer was the sole reason for walking into the village that afternoon. Mrs Gaskell did not mind, though, she was happy to be presented with the opportunity to stretch her legs after the long journey, and Charlotte was happy to show her friend around the village.

After purchasing dripping at the butchers and bread, flour and yeast from the bakers, the two writers progressed to Mr Greenwood's shop and stepped inside. The proprietor was always happy to see Charlotte, and the fact that she should be accompanied that day by Mrs Elizabeth Gaskell, a writer whose books he had sold in his shop, thrilled him.

'A double pleasure indeed…' Mr Greenwood enthused. 'Two famous writers in my establishment together.' He shook the ladies' hands, and then a thought struck suddenly and he turned sharply to Charlotte. 'I trust you'll not take off with your friend, Miss Brontë, and set up residence in Manchester. For I'd be put out of business in days without the patronage of my best customer.'

'You exaggerate, Mr Greenwood, I'm sure,' Charlotte replied. 'But no, I have no present plan to leave Haworth. Unless, in the unlikely event, a proposition is put before me that I am unable to refuse.'

Laughter erupted.

While it was true that Charlotte's custom provided the stationer with a useful income, requiring a constant supply of writing paper, ink, pencils, pen nibs and envelopes, Haworth was a bustling village and Charlotte was in no doubt that his business would survive without her custom. Mr Greenwood, though, was delighted when Charlotte and Mrs Gaskell made significant purchases before leaving.

Dinner was served normally at one o'clock, but in order to accommodate their guest, dinner that day was served at six o'clock – the time that tea was usually taken. A minute past the given hour, for either, and Tabby's wrath would be served at a temperature greater than the food.

Mr Brontë joined Charlotte and Mrs Gaskell at the table. Martha carried in the cutlery and a plate of bread and butter. Tabby, carrying the casserole pot between both hands, using a towel to protect them from the heat, followed close behind and, after dishing up the chicken casserole, she and Martha left the diners in peace to enjoy their meal. Prayers were said and dinner commenced.

Mrs Gaskell enjoyed every mouthful, claiming that the chicken casserole was tastier than the food prepared by her own cook. Mr Brontë, having had an eye on the last crust of bread for some minutes, hoped desperately that no one else might desire it, and indeed, the ladies' opportunity was lost in a flash. Unable to resist any longer, his hand shot out and snatched the last remaining crust from the plate. He turned to both Charlotte and Mrs Gaskell, smiling guiltily but neither seemed to mind.

'You'll find the village folk rather odd, I dare say, Lily?' He said, chewing on the spoils. 'Rude and rough compared with the cultured people of Manchester?'

'Not everyone in Manchester is cultured, Mr Brontë,' Mrs Gaskell said with alacrity, putting down her spoon. 'And whether the people of Haworth are rough and odd is not for me to judge. I confess, though, that everyone I have so far met seems quite unique, and I can see now from where Charlotte's characters are drawn.'

'Aye, some, certainly,' Mr Brontë said, chuckling. 'The men folk on the farms are a particularly vulgar lot, as rough and tough as the rocks on the moor.'

'I dare say there's an element of truth in that, Mr Brontë,' Mrs Gaskell said, and then she turned from him. 'Indeed, Charlotte, I'm not at all surprised you remain unmarried, for there seems a distinct lack of suitable suitors in Haworth.'

Charlotte smiled, if nervously, and the words had barely left Mrs Gaskell's lips, when Mr Brontë allowed the spoon to fall onto his plate, and he slid the chair on which he sat backwards noisily along the floor, and he stood up abruptly.

'Excuse me,' he said, chewing still. 'I have work to attend to, and you ladies, I'm sure, will have matters to discuss that are unfit for my ears.'

His stern glare and abruptness of manner unsettled Mrs Gaskell. With a look of dread she watched him leave the room, and then she turned sharply to Charlotte, mortified.

'I'm dreadfully sorry, Charlotte, I've hardly been here five minutes and I've caused offence already.'

'No, Lily, you've offended no one,' Charlotte assured her, touching Mrs Gaskell's hand and smiling reassuringly. 'I apologise for my father's rudeness, but you are not at fault. It's me who offends, not you.'

'You!' Mrs Gaskell said, askance; and then a smile broke slowly upon her lips. 'Not Mr Arthur Bell Nicholls!'

'He, indeed, Lily. After considering the things you said when I visited last, I decided to act,' she said and smiled, sighing in her next breath. 'Unfortunately, striking up a relationship with the *lowly* curate riled Papa like you would not believe.'

'Well… your father is perhaps afraid.'

'Afraid!'

'Of being abandoned, left alone in this bleak place.'

'But the servants will be here still.'

'I dare say they will, but it's not the same as having a loving daughter around. Work your charm on him, Charlotte; your father's resolve will soften given time, I'm sure. It's natural for fathers to be protective of their children, it's admirable and understandable, but do not let him ruin what might be your one real chance of matrimonial happiness. A genuine offer of marriage, from a sincere and caring man does not come one's way every day.'

It rained for much of the time that Mrs Gaskell stayed at the parsonage, delaying an expressed wish to walk on the moors and see for herself the wild and rugged landscape. But on the day prior to her departure, the clouds parted, the rain ceased and the sun broke through. After rising early and breakfasting, Charlotte and Mrs Gaskell were soon in their stride, walking across the moors with Flossy running at their sides.

'How vast it all is,' Mrs Gaskell enthused, upon reaching a high point after an exhausting climb, halting and looking out over the surrounding hills. 'From a distance, and especially under leaden skies, the moors look moody and bleak, but once the sun is upon them they are majestically transformed and the view is truly magnificent. One can see for miles – and only scant wisps of polluting smoke rising from the chimneys of the farmsteads scattered about the hills.'

'Oh, but you should come again in August, Lily. The heather is in bloom then, and the moors are transformed yet again: a sea of purple for as far as the eye can see; a truly spectacular sight, and the air is perfumed with the delicate scent of the heather.'

'In some districts of Manchester, one is fortunate to see anything at all through the fog. Smoke hangs heavy in the air and every breath tastes foul and acrid, and then there's the poverty...'

'We have our share of poverty in Haworth and many other social issues. Papa strives constantly to improve sanitation... improve the quality of the drinking water, but progress is painfully slow.'

'Well, in Haworth you are able to escape to the moors, drink the clean water from the streams.'

'Indeed, and Emily would do that,' Charlotte said and smiled. 'When we were children, the moors were our home as much as the parsonage. Emily would have lived in a cave were she able. She liked nothing better than charging about the heath with the dogs running at her side. She was forever messing about in ponds and streams – up to her elbows in water and mud, she cared not. Womanly virtues meant little or nothing to Emily. She would seek out small fish, or any creature she knew would terrify me and thrust it in my face, and laugh until she was giddy. She had the strength of an ox, the tenacity of a man and could climb any tree with ease, scramble fearlessly over jagged rocks that hard men shied away from. Yet she could play the piano beautifully – strike every note with exact precision. Poor, dear Emily... so much life and energy and then...'

'Poor, Charlotte,' Mrs Gaskell said, drawing her tight to her. 'You must miss Emily terribly, Anne also?'

Charlotte smiled. 'Ah, yes, Anne... when Emily played the piano Anne would sing along. Her voice was sublime, sweeter than a choir of angels – Papa loved nothing better than to sit quietly of an evening and listen to Anne singing while Emily played the piano. You would have liked Anne best of all, Lily, I'm sure. She was kind and sweet... delicate and fragile – altogether unlike Emily. A day never passes when I do not think of my sisters, but in August, I think most of Anne, for in the purple mists I see the violet tint of her eyes. You never saw eyes like Anne's...'

A cloud blotted out the sun, and they looked up together. Mrs Gaskell shivered and when she returned her gaze to Charlotte, she noticed that her eyes had misted over. She drew Charlotte tighter to her.

'Perhaps we should turn back?'

'But we've walked little more than a mile and a half, and there's so much more to see.'

'Another day, Charlotte... the moors grow cold quickly once the sun has disappeared,' Mrs Gaskell said, glancing to the sky once again. 'And I fear it will not shine upon us again today.'

'You are right, Lily... better if we cut short our pleasure than catch a chill.' She said and smiled. 'The pity is that you must leave in the morning. It's been wonderful – such a tonic having a friend to stay with interests and views similar to mine.' The two friends turned and headed for home. 'But it's right that you should return home to your children... you must miss them terribly; and your four girls will be missing their mother, Julia especially.'

'Ah, yes,' Mrs Gaskell said, smiling distractedly. 'My girls... but Marianne does a splendid job looking after Julia.

She'll make a wonderful mother one day, as I'm sure would you, Charlotte!'

Charlotte smiled. 'Well… you will visit again, won't you, Lily?'

'Of course I will,' Mrs Gaskell said. She paused. 'In August,' she added and laughed. 'By then I'll be desperate to escape the polluted Manchester air; be ready to purge my lungs again in the invigorating moorland air of Yorkshire and inhale the perfume of the heather.'

Before leaving Haworth, Mrs Gaskell reiterated, to Charlotte, the importance of trusting in her own feelings, and marrying Mr Nicholls if she so wished. If it upset her father, that could be dealt with and overcome on another day.

Chapter Twenty-Six

One frosty January morning, Martha handed Charlotte a letter. She glanced at the handwriting and smiled, tearing open the envelope as she climbed up the stairs. She removed the letter from the sleeve and opened it out in the privacy of her room, and then her face exploded with delight:

"Dearest Charlotte,

Next week I shall be staying with the Grants in Oxenhope. On Wednesday I shall walk along the pathway toward Haworth and wait by the sycamore trees. I will be there at two o'clock and will wait for half an hour. If you are able to come, my darling, wrap up well in warm clothing. Your loving friend, Arthur…"

Charlotte had not seen Mr Nicholls in months and she was desperate to see him again. Struggling to contain her emotions, she threw herself onto her bed on her back and read the letter again and again. Overwhelmed and dizzy with unimaginable joy, the ceiling, the entire room seemed to rotate. But reality struck and cut short her euphoria: her father would never approve. Charlotte knew that if she wished to see Mr Nicholls, the meeting would have to be conducted in secret.

It snowed for much of the said morning and it was typical that Tabby should be irritable and in bad humour. Then the reason became apparent: the cooking range was slow and dinner would be late. Charlotte, eager to know at what hour dinner would be ready, tested the servant's patience with persistent questioning, repeatedly urging her to speed things up.

Dinner was served half an hour late, and afterwards Mr Brontë, impatient to know what progress had been made with initiatives put forward by him regarding the quality of drinking water, summoned the assistance of Charlotte to read to him an article from the newspaper.

Charlotte was twenty minutes late when she sneaked out from the parsonage. Several inches of snow covered the ground; the path was treacherous and every attempt to hurry, produced the opposite effect, causing her to slip and slide and stumble. Added to that, the people she encountered wished to detain her and talk: every barrier possible, it seemed, had been put in her way to prevent the tryst with Mr Nicholls from taking place. The Lord, Charlotte thought, had perhaps intervened in order to prevent her from falling into disreputable ways.

On the path between Oxenhope and Haworth, stood the hopeful curate, a lonely figure against the vast white canvas. The leafless sycamore trees he shuffled beneath offered little by way of shelter from the wind, or from the falling snow.

Stamping his feet and rubbing his hands together, Mr Nicholls looked constantly about for Charlotte through eyes that wept from the bitter sting of the wind. His nose and cheeks looked on fire; and he jumped up and down and stamped his feet like he was angry, and Mr Nicholls was angry; he was angry with himself for his selfishness. For attempting to tempt Charlotte away from a warm fire in order that he might feast his eyes upon her for a few snatched moments. Jumping up and down, clapping his hands together and slapping his breast, he tried everything he could to restore warmth and feeling to a frozen body, to limbs stiffened almost to petrification from the cold. Sighing, he thrust a hand inside his coat and pulled out his watch and flipped open the case: Charlotte was thirty-five minutes late. The wind blew stronger, the sky darkened and the snow fell heavier. Charlotte would not come now, he knew; but he would hang on for a few more minutes, just in case.

He waited for five more minutes, until his body trembled uncontrollably and he could stand the cold no longer. Frozen and dejected, he turned and headed for his friend's home in Oxenhope. Walking slowly at first, turning periodically back, hoping and praying, but Charlotte was no fool, he knew. She was an intelligent woman, blessed with more sense than to endanger her life and walk out into the virulent blizzard. Mr Nicholls lowered his head and then strode purposely away: thoughts of a hot drink and a warm fire quickened his step.

Disturbed snow and vague footprints were visible still when Charlotte, breathless and covered in snow, arrived at the same spot on the path where minutes earlier Mr Nicholls had stood. She looked about, smiling hopefully and then she followed the imprecise imprints half expecting that Mr Nicholls would leap out from behind a wall or a tree and surprise her. He did not and the further Charlotte walked the more despondent she became. The snow fell heavier and the wind blew stronger, filling in every trace of her lover's footprints. Charlotte halted and shouted out Mr Nicholls' name and listened; she called out several times, but no reply was returned. But her soft voice, would not carry far in the heavy atmosphere, even if he had been within range.

Charlotte was soaked to the skin; she was frozen and a tremor began that would not be stilled. In utter frustration, and through chattering teeth, she screamed out Mr Nicholls' name one last time, but the hoped-for voice was not returned. Nothing stirred or was heard except for a flock of bleating sheep seeking shelter from the snow. Miserable and deflated, Charlotte tightened her clothing, turned and headed for home.

Chapter Twenty-Seven

Breathless, covered in snow and shivering, Charlotte opened the parsonage door as quietly as she was able and then tiptoed inside. Her stealth, though, was in vain; thwarted when Flossy raced out from the kitchen, barking to rouse the entire household and beyond.

'Is that you, Charlotte?' Mr Brontë called sternly from his study.

Charlotte winced. 'It is, Papa.'

'Where on earth!' shrieked Tabby, as she hobbled out from the kitchen, wiping her hands on her pinafore, shuffling hurriedly toward Charlotte. 'Wet through and trembling… come here, woman,' she beseeched, reaching out and unbuttoning Charlotte's coat, tugging the snow-covered garment from her.

'What need was there to be out?' Her father demanded. 'Risking your health in the blizzard! You ought to know better.'

'I, I was out of writing paper.'

'Writing paper!' Tabby repeated disparagingly, as her eyes searched for the said package. She grimaced and shook her head.

'Couldn't it have waited until another day?' Mr Brontë said, and then in his next breath added perversely. 'You could at least have taken the dog out with you.'

'Yes, Papa, yes, yes, yes,' Charlotte mocked in a whispered tone.

Tabby stood glaring, waiting for Charlotte to take off her bonnet and scarf. Snatching them from her and, after shaking the snow from them over the doormat, she hung them on the coat stand. Charlotte, standing watching, smiled affectionately.

'Dear old Tabby—'

'Old!' Tabby barked.

Charlotte's smile widened. 'How would we manage without you?'

Tabby remained silent, standing glaring, resting her hands on her hips, shaking her head.

'Well… will you take yourself off upstairs?' the servant said. 'And get out of your wet undergarments, or shall I undress you like a baby!'

'You may undress me, Tabby, but only if you'll dry me with a warm towel and then powder my bottom,' Charlotte said, and ran up the stairs, giggling.

'Impertinent…' Tabby called after her, shaking her head and chuckling. 'I'll have a blazing fire ready when you come back down… a mug of beef tea.'

Charlotte turned. 'Dear old, Tabby,' she said again, and laughed.

Snow fell throughout the remainder of the day, it fell well into the night, but come morning the clouds had dispersed, leaving behind a clear sky. Only the wind remained, a cold and penetrating wind that blew incessantly from a north-easterly direction. Charlotte, sitting huddled by the fire in the dining room, writing, appeared unconcerned by the weather. At intervals she rose and stoked the fire, stretched her limbs and walked up to the window and looked outside. Oxenhope was not far away; and she imagined herself imprisoned in a castle and Mr Nicholls striding through the deep snow to rescue her; or riding on the back of a black whinnying stallion, declaring his love for her and beseeching her father grant him her hand. Of course he did neither.

Yesterday's missed tryst was foremost in Charlotte's mind, and she would walk today, she decided, to the same place at the same hour and hope and pray that Mr Nicholls might think alike.

Dinner was served at the appropriate hour and Charlotte had the luxury of time and tidied away her morning's work. When two o'clock approached, she put on her scarf, bonnet and coat in the hall but, as she crept toward the exit, the study door opened. Her father's eyes widened.

'You're surely not walking out today!'

'I must—'

'Must! After the soaking you suffered yesterday.'

'I suffered nothing yesterday, and in any case the sun is shining today.'

'No matter, the wind is bitter still and the sky has begun to cloud over. I fear we'll have more snow before the day is out. For what purpose must you go out?'

'I, I… ink… I am out of ink.'

Mr Brontë smiled. 'Then take off your coat, Charlotte, for I possess a little ink. You may use mine.'

'Thank you, Papa, but, but yours will not do.'

'Not do!'

Charlotte opened the door. 'Yours is a different shade to mine, and my publisher demands conformity.'

'Conf—'

'Goodbye, Papa,' Charlotte said and then hurried out, slamming the door behind her. Her father winced and started.

'Confound it!' he retorted, standing open-mouthed and staring at the closed door. 'Confound your foolishness!' He shouted out after her.

Charlotte, hearing his voice as she descended the steps, turned back and smiled and then hurried away along the garden path, through the gate and along the lane. Despite having time to spare earlier, she was now several minutes late.

Chapter Twenty-Eight

Mr Nicholls stood in the same place at the same hour, hunched and rubbing his hands together, shuffling his feet, turning his head one way and then another. He took out his watch and checked the time, shook his head and then returned the watch to his pocket. Though the day was fine, the wind cut through the heavy overcoat he wore and tore into his flesh; indeed the day was not at all conducive to standing long in an exposed country lane. He shivered, his teeth chattered and his breath was visible in the arctic air like steam rising from a boiling kettle: he would not hang about long today, he decided.

Ten, fifteen more minutes passed and Mr Nicholls, frozen and dejected, turned and began to walk slowly away. Perhaps Charlotte had never intended to come anyway, he thought, or maybe she had been prevented. He tightened his collar, thrust his hands deep inside his coat pockets, lengthened his stride and quickened his pace.

'Wait! Mr Nicholls, please wait!'

The music he longed to hear. A warming glow rippled through his body, banishing the cold in an instant. Turning abruptly round, he slipped on the icy surface and almost fell over. But it would not have mattered had he lain prostrate in the snow for an hour; he would not have felt its sting. His face beamed, as Charlotte, waving fervently, hastened toward him. In her eagerness, she stumbled too.

'Careful, my love, careful…'

They were together at last. Standing face-to-face, gazing into each other's eyes, breathless and speechless and unable to steal their eyes away from one another. Charlotte spoke first.

'Oh, Arthur, I'm sorry, I almost missed you again.'

'Well, you are here.'

'It was such a trial leaving home with so many eyes upon me.'

'Well, I, I…' Mr Nicholls' stuttered. He was lost for words, as his disbelieving eyes continued to gaze upon her face. He reached out, took her gloved hand tentatively into his, lifted it up to his lips and kissed her fingers. 'I can hardly believe that you are really here, Charlotte. It's like a dream; one that I hope never to awaken from.'

'Poor Arthur… hanging about in the cold, just so we can be together for a few snatched minutes,' she said, lowering her gaze. 'Have you no gloves? Your hands must be frozen!'

'Worry not for me, Charlotte, your presence puts a fire in my spirits. Its magic works its way into my fingertips and warms them.'

'I cannot stay long, Arthur, I'm afraid. Papa thinks I've slipped out to purchase ink.'

'That you could come at all puts me in ecstasies; and if it's for a few minutes only it will indeed do,' he said, taking hold of Charlotte, drawing her cautiously to him. When she smiled, he hugged her tighter, he kissed her cheek, and when her smile widened, he kissed her lips.

'Arthur…!'

'There, Charlotte, I've dreamed of that moment; I've practiced it in my mind a thousand times since the day I first saw you.'

Charlotte smiled and touched her lips. 'I—'

'You shiver from the cold, my love. Let's walk… in the direction of your home, and then when we part you'll not have far to go.'

'Dear, Arthur… so thoughtful and kind…'

They walked to the graveyard of Charlotte's father's church and sheltered beneath the hanging boughs of a yew tree. Mr Brontë would not to see them there should he have a mind to venture out. Mr Nicholls unfastened his coat, opened it out and enveloped Charlotte inside it, warming her with his body.

They stood in silence for a while, gazing into the other's eyes and then Mr Nicholls leaned slowly closer and pressed his cheek gently against Charlotte's. She gasped, feeling his cold cheek against hers. His warm breaths on her neck shot a pleasing tingling sensation the length of her spine.

'Oh, Arthur…' Charlotte said and sighed, backing away from him, looking deep into his eyes, appearing unsure whether to smile or feign shock at the intimacy of the moment, but she smiled. Mr Nicholls reciprocated and he, accepting her acquiescence as a signal of approval, instilled in him the confidence to swamp her lips with more kisses, with passionate kisses, kisses that lingered.

'Arthur…! Charlotte said and gulped, holding him from her, but smiling. 'Such, such—'

He silenced her mouth with yet more kisses, and then Charlotte, gasping for breath, stopped him and stepped back. She lifted a hand up to her lips, as her eyes searched his face.

'There…' he said. 'Had you reason to doubt my sincerity, well, you now know—'

'I must hurry home,' she said, flustered suddenly and moving further away from him.

Mr Nicholls smiled, if somewhat uncertainly, fearing that his spontaneity, and his ardent behaviour might have been a little too hasty. Deflated, he began fastening the buttons on his coat. But he need not have doubted Charlotte's feelings for him, nor of her desire for, while he was thus distracted and deep in thought, she darted forward, sprung up on tiptoe and kissed his lips with a passion to outdo his. Astonished, Mr Nicholls' eyes widened, and he smiled.

'Darling Charlotte,' he said, his eyes searching her face. 'I'll cherish that kiss until we next meet.'

Charlotte was not done, though and when he returned his attention to the buttons, she launched herself at him once again, kissing his lips with greater fervour than before. Now it was Mr Nicholls' turn to gulp.

'Charlotte, I, I—!'

'There, Arthur… for me, the next time cannot come soon enough.'

Mr Nicholls, after catching his breath, gathered Charlotte into his arms and kissed her forehead. 'You tremble from the cold, my love, you must hurry home.'

'The cold affects me no more, Arthur,' she said and laughed. 'But you are right, Papa will be anxious if I do not return home soon.'

'Indeed, Charlotte, hurry home and thaw out the ink,' Mr Nicholls said and laughed. Charlotte laughed and then she rested her head against his breast.

'Poor Arthur, I have no distance to walk at all, but you have far,' she said, pausing and sighing. 'Oh, Arthur… if only Papa knew how much we meant to each other. Right now he seems intent on seeing you as nothing other than an opportunist – a fortune hunter.'

'Well… his opposition will perhaps soften one day,' Mr Nicholls said and smiled. He stroked her face. 'Your cheeks are like ice, Charlotte. Ask Tabby to make you a mug of beef tea when you reach home.'

'Dear old Tabby, she'll have had a mug of beef tea waiting for me this past hour and more.'

'Well, hurry home, my love, for if illness should impose its presence, your father's determination to keep us apart will only strengthen.'

Reluctantly, the two lovers parted. They stepped out from beneath the yew tree and walked in their respective opposite directions, turning periodically back, calling to each other and waving.

The wind blew fiercer and Mr Nicholls pulled his collar tighter about his neck. Despite the bitter wind, though, he was jubilant and smiling and strode through the deep snow toward Oxenhope, dismissive of the snow that had now begun to blow in on the strengthening wind.

Over the next few days Mr Nicholls and Charlotte met several times; they met on every subsequent occasion he had reason, or excuse, to stay with the Grant family in Oxenhope. But again the secrecy made Charlotte feel wretched; she hated deceiving her father, but she was in love and desperate to secure his approval, desperate to be able to conduct her relationship openly with Mr Nicholls – show off her beau to the world, and let everyone see and judge for themselves. The time spent in Mr Nicholls' company had convinced Charlotte of his devotion to her, of his sincerity: no man could love her more, and her affection for Mr Nicholls strengthened each time that they met. It strengthened her belief that, if she could only make her father understand how happy Mr Nicholls had made her, he would surely deny her no longer.

Sitting at the breakfast table one morning with her father, Charlotte stirred the porridge in the bowl on the table in front of her, but with little desire to taste it. She was nervous, hot and her heart beat a heightened rhythm. Looking nervously to him, she took a deep breath and then released the spoon in the dish.

'Papa,' she blurted, 'in a few days' time Mr Nicholls will be staying with the Grant family in Oxenhope—'

'What of it?'

'It's my wish to see him.'

Mr Brontë jumped up out of his chair. 'Why seek my permission if your mind is already made up?'

'Arthur and I would prefer to conduct our friendship with your approval.'

Mr Brontë glared. 'Nicholls will never gain my approval, Charlotte, not ever.'

'But, Papa, Mr Nicholls is a principled man of tolerable good sense, you know he is and he, he…' She halted as her eyes searched his thunderous face. 'He loves me, Papa, really and truly.'

'Love, bah! Find another man, Charlotte; Nicholls is not good enough.'

'I want no other man,' she shouted.

Mr Brontë gasped; he slumped down in his chair, tugging his cravat. A look of horror distorted Charlotte's features as he began to struggle for breath. She went to his aid and unwound his cravat.

'Do as you wish, Charlotte,' he snapped, waving her away. 'But speak no more to me of Nicholls, and let him not come near my home.'

'But Papa!'

'Papa, nothing,' he cut in, growling and waving his arms about. He jumped up and knocked over a pot of coffee. 'Martha!'

Martha, flustered, looked inside the dining room; she

saw the spilt drink and retreated, returning promptly armed with a bucket and a cloth. In his haste to leave, Mr Brontë almost collided with her in the doorway. Gesticulating, he offered muted apology and then shuffled hurriedly away. Martha, open-mouthed and watching, turned to Charlotte once he had disappeared inside his study.

'I've not seen Mr Brontë in such a temper before.'

'No, Martha,' Charlotte said. 'And nor did I think him capable of such rage until… well, never mind.'

Charlotte's mind was set. She was determined not to let her father's obstinacy stand in the way of her happiness. Her relationship with Mr Nicholls would continue whatever his theatricals – whatever he might say or think. Mr Nicholls loved her and she loved him, nothing could be more certain. It was she, not her father, who would live with the consequences if her judgement were proved wrong.

Charlotte and Mr Nicholls continued to meet over the coming months. They walked on the moors together, they walked openly about the village, but Charlotte respected her father's wish and did not speak to him of Mr Nicholls. She kept her lover away from the parsonage and out of sight of her father, which, to her, seemed churlish since everyone in Haworth knew and approved of their friendship. People stopped them in the street and congratulated them on their engagement, but it seemed that if Charlotte wished to marry Mr Nicholls, it would be without her father's blessing.

Chapter Twenty-Nine

Miracles are rare, but confirmation that they can occasionally occur came by way of Mr Brontë's unexpected change of mind. As improbable as it might seem, all opposition to Charlotte and Mr Nicholls marrying was, without explanation, suddenly withdrawn. They were free to go ahead and marry with his full blessing, and should anyone have cause to doubt Mr Brontë's sincerity and generosity, it was reinforced when he reinstated Mr Nicholls at his church as his curate.

Mr Brontë's volte-face impacted upon himself as much as anyone: gone were the brooding looks, his abruptness of tone; his manner was more agreeable and he went about the village smiling readily at everyone he met. He was relaxed and conversed enthusiastically with his parishioners regarding the forthcoming marriage of his daughter to Mr Nicholls, whether they wished to hear of it or they did not. Charlotte was happier; the headaches and nausea that had blighted her life were less frequent, her step was lighter and she, too, went about the village with a smile on her lips.

Sitting cleaning her spectacles by the fire one day, Charlotte appeared oblivious to the hailstones battering the windows. She put on her spectacles, and picked up her pen.

"Dearest Nell,

That which not long ago seemed impossible is arranged. I am engaged to Mr Nicholls and will be married 29th June."

Ellen's eyes widened, but instead of the expected favourable response, a look of dread, anger even, darkened her features. Swallowing hard, she turned to her mother, resting on the sofa next to Mercy.

'You'll not believe it, Mama, but Charlotte is engaged to be married—'

'Engaged! To who?'

'Mr Arthur Bell Nicholls.' Ellen spoke firmly and with an air of contempt and then her eyes consumed the remainder of the letter. 'And listen to this, Mama; listen to what Charlotte says: "Providence has put this proposition before me and I'm sure it's for the best". Providence, huh! Nicholls' scheming more like has turned her head. What of her pact of spinsterhood!' Ellen retorted, turning again to her mother. 'That man, Mama, is determined to destroy mine and Charlotte's friendship. Nicholls manipulates her; she is his puppet and will do or say whatever he tells her to.'

'Dear me, Ellen,' Mrs Nussey began. 'You are mistaken, I'm sure. Charlotte must love Mr Nicholls, or she would not have agreed to marry him.'

'Charlotte says Mr Nicholls loves her, but not once has she spoken of *her* love for *him*.'

It was perhaps understandable that Ellen should be upset; she and Charlotte had been friends since school, they were like sisters, forming a bond that had continued and strengthened with the passing years – more so after the deaths of Charlotte's siblings. Each other's home was their home and many days and hours had been spent in each other's company. Marriage, Ellen knew, would change all that and she feared that change. Charlotte would no longer be in control of her own affairs; she would be obliged to obey – surrender to her husband's desires, to his demands. Everything that Charlotte wished to do would require the endorsement of her husband. If Charlotte wished to visit, she would first have to consult her husband; he would say if and when Charlotte could visit; he would say if and when she could visit Charlotte. Marital obligations, Ellen knew, would take precedence over all else. Yet Ellen knew that Charlotte was no fool; she was not blind and would know what she was entering into with marriage.

But would she?

How often, when dazzled by the thrill of a new romance, distracted by the consuming sensuousness of that lustful first flush, unattractive habits remain concealed, and those few that surface are nullified by the intoxicating effects of love. Emerging only after the snare has clasped shut to reveal the terrifying ugliness of incompatibility.

Mr Brontë shuffled into the dining room. Charlotte looked to him and smiled; she removed her spectacles, stood up and went to his side. She took his arm into hers and guided him to his chair by the fire and then lowered him into it.

'Dearest, Papa,' she gushed. 'You cannot imagine how happy you've made me – you've made Arthur very happy. Life, the air I breathe, the water I drink, and the food I eat tastes infinitely sweeter. Headaches and sickness hardly trouble me at all'

'Well… it's good you have reason to rejoice.'

'My destiny as Mrs Nicholls might not be a brilliant one, but I do love Arthur, or I would not marry him. And Arthur loves me, I know he does, and if marrying him brings only a modicum of happiness back into my life, it will indeed do.'

'To be sure, Charlotte, but, but—'

'Without your approval, Arthur and I would not have been half as happy.'

'Indeed, but, but there's still time to change your mind,'

Mr Brontë said, gesticulating uncomfortably and adding. 'And it's good you'll have the chance to visit friends one last time. You'll then have time to reflect – decide if marriage is right for you. Mrs Gaskell will know all that there is to know about married life – from a woman's perspective. She'll be able to advise and guide you, and you'll likely see things clearer. Married life doesn't suit everyone, Charlotte.'

'My mind is settled, Papa. Indeed, it was Lily who instilled in me the confidence to follow my own heart.'

'Lily did!' Mr Brontë said, his eyes widening.

'Lily's marriage to William is happy and fulfilling; and she speaks with much enthusiasm of her family, and especially of her four girls. You should see them, Papa, they truly are adorable, Julia especially.'

'Children, well…' Mr Brontë uttered, turning thoughtful.

It seemed ironic that Mrs Gaskell should have given Charlotte encouragement to marry when Mr Brontë had hoped that, had she been the one to explain to his daughter the minutiae of expected conjugal obligations that come with marriage, Charlotte might have baulked and found such intimacy with a man distasteful and dissuaded her from marrying. Mr Brontë knew also how Charlotte valued her liberty; travelling and visiting friends whenever she pleased: that would all end with marriage. But a union between Charlotte and Mr Nicholls now seemed inevitable. Mr Brontë knew it; outwardly he welcomed it, but inwardly he feared it.

Chapter Thirty

As Charlotte prepared to set out on one last journey as a single woman, Tabby fussed over her, checking and re-checking that everything she needed had been attended to.

'Thank you, Tabby, but I've already got a light rug for my knees. It's summer, for heaven's sake! Let me be.' Charlotte protested, when the elderly servant attempted to force another garment upon her – another blanket to cover her legs.

'You'll have to do as you are bid once you're married.'

'Pray, Tabby, please do not make marriage sound so despotic and unyielding, for I am sure it is not,' Charlotte said, and then she smiled. 'Indeed, I cannot wait to be married to Arthur.'

'He'll put a stop to your gallivanting, for sure: London one week, Birstall and then Manchester—'

'Arthur will perhaps wish to accompany me,' Charlotte said cheerfully. 'In fact I should quite like to take him to Manchester, show him off to Lily. Her husband is a church minister and Arthur and Mr Gaskell would get along admirably, I'm sure – they'd find much in common to talk about.'

'I wish I could go to Manchester, Miss,' Martha said dreamily, as she squeezed a bag of biscuits into Charlotte's handbag. Biscuits that Tabby had baked earlier that morning and were a treat for Mrs Gaskell's children. 'All those people and things—'

'Aye!' Tabby cut in. 'Black smoke billowing from scores of mill chimneys choking the streets. Damp, polluted air, noise and squalor – crime!' Frowning, she shook her head. 'I'm afraid Manchester wouldn't do for me at all.'

'Manchester's not half as bad as you make out, Tabby,' Charlotte said. 'In fact there's little by way of pollution or poverty in Plymouth Grove where Mrs Gaskell lives.'

Martha was not deterred. 'Well I'm sure I'd like Manchester.'

'One day perhaps, Martha; when Arthur and I have children, we'll need a nanny to accompany us.'

Mr Brontë's eyes widened and; grimacing and shaking his head, he ambled into the hall, faced his daughter and smiled.

'Your carriage awaits, Charlotte.'

That was Tabby's cue; hobbling unwieldy toward Charlotte, she began adjusting her coat, her bonnet and her scarf.

'For heaven's sake, Tabby…'

'Keep still, will you, Miss Brontë – you were much less trouble when you were a bairn – can't have you catching a chill with your wedding day so near,' Tabby said, looking intently at Charlotte. She shook her head. 'And how I'll ever get used to calling you Mrs Nicholls after the years as Miss Charlotte Brontë, I don't know!' She stepped away, sighed and then lunged forward. 'Come here,' she said, and then enveloped Charlotte in a tight embrace, hugging her like an overzealous mother might on seeing her daughter set out on an uncertain journey.

Charlotte did mull over all that her father had said earlier, all that she had been the unwilling recipient of, giving due consideration to the suitability of married life. Marrying Mr Nicholls, she felt certain, was absolutely the right thing to do. It would change her life, Charlotte knew it, and she welcomed that change. She could hardly wait until the day they were married… immerse herself in the fulfilling and rewarding domestic life that she felt marriage would offer, to the new and exciting experiences: the intimacy of living with a man, and of having a man to love and care for and for a man to return that love. Arthur loved her, Charlotte was certain, and she loved him: there were no doubts, no buts. Nothing could possibly stand in her way. In a few weeks' time she would no longer be Charlotte Brontë, she would be Mrs Charlotte Nicholls.

Chapter Thirty-One

Mrs Gaskell was delighted that Charlotte should make the time for one last visit before her marriage, and the instant she saw the carriage pull up outside her home she rushed out to meet her.

'Oh, Charlotte, what joy!' Mrs Gaskell enthused, hugging and kissing the soon-to-be-bride, taking her arm and escorting her along the path to her home. 'When I read your letter I struggled to believe it! Married – and to Mr Nicholls. I, like you, had thought it a hopeless case.'

'Indeed, Lily, and pinch my flesh of a morning, for it feels like I am dreaming still.'

The coachman followed carrying Charlotte's suitcases and, as instructed, he left them in the hall; received his fare and then departed, wishing Charlotte a pleasant stay.

Mrs Gaskell's four girls came running into the hall and gathered around Charlotte, greeting her with hugs and kisses. Julia appeared reluctant to let go of Charlotte's coat, and clung on, releasing it only when Charlotte reached inside her bag.

'Let me see now… see what I've brought for you, beautiful girls,' she said, lifting a brown paper bag from her handbag and handing it to Marianne, the eldest girl. 'Tabby baked them especially for you four girls.'

Marianne's face beamed, as did the faces of her sisters when she thrust the bag of biscuits under the noses of each.

'Take one biscuit each,' their mother cut in, 'and then hand the remainder to the servant to put in the pantry until later.'

'But she might eat them,' Julia complained, biscuit crumbs spilling from her lips as she chewed.

'Please don't speak with your mouth full, Julia,' the girl's mother admonished mildly, smiling with her next breath. 'But if the servant eats them, then Miss Brontë will have to honour us with another visit, won't she?' She said, turning to Charlotte, her smile widening. 'And if she brings a husband, they'll be able to carry twice as many biscuits.'

The girls cheered.

'Are you getting married, Miss?' Florence asked.

'I've already told you she is,' her mother reminded her. 'Now, run along girls and play; Miss Brontë and I have much to discuss.'

The girls raced excitedly away chatting and chewing; Mrs Gaskell looked on with fondness and then she steered Charlotte into the living room and invited her to sit next to her on the sofa. The servant entered soon after pushing a trolley with a teapot, cups, saucers and a selection of cakes arranged on tiered plates. She transferred the refreshments and cakes to the coffee table, poured the tea and, after enquiring if anything else was needed, pushed the trolley away and left the two writers alone to talk.

Charlotte was thirsty and had lifted the cup and saucer from the table almost immediately after it had been set down in front of her. Mrs Gaskell's eye followed the cup from its saucer up to Charlotte's lips, and she smiled.

'You positively bloom, Charlotte,' she said. 'The prospect of marrying, it seems, works its magic on you already.'

Charlotte smiled, nervously and then set the cup clumsily back on its saucer and lowered it back down onto the coffee table. She turned to Mrs Gaskell, bearing a concerned expression.

'And I look forward to the day when Arthur and I are married,' Charlotte began. 'But nerves get the better of me and, at times, I wonder if I'm doing the right thing.'

'Dear me, Charlotte…' Mrs Gaskell said, chuckling and shuffling round on the sofa, taking Charlotte's hands into hers. 'Doubts are bound to surface as the big day approaches. It was the same for me, it's the same for everyone, I'm sure, but if it feels right in your heart—'

'And it does.'

'Then worry no more, Charlotte. Lingering doubts will dissipate once the theatricals of marrying are over and done with,' Mrs Gaskell reassured her. She paused and then smiled. 'But tell me, how did you manage to sway your father?'

'I know not how, Lily; one minute Papa would not hear of Arthur's name spoken from my lips, and in the next all opposition to marrying him had mysteriously vanished. What persuaded Papa to change his mind I cannot tell; and I felt it unwise to question him. Now, Papa will hear no ill spoken of Arthur. I am happy, Arthur is happy, but Papa appears the happiest of all. I cannot understand it!'

'Your troubles are over, Charlotte.'

The two writers sat for a moment in silence, eating cakes and sipping tea, but Charlotte appeared uneasy and nervous still, shuffling and looking about, staring abstractedly through eyes widened with unsettling thoughts for her future. And then she cleared her throat and turned.

'The one thing troubling me most yet, Lily, is the thought of lying in bed next to a man. It will indeed seem strange.'

'Strange!'

'I've only ever before lain in bed with my sisters and my friend, Ellen Nussey.'

'Worry not, Charlotte, for if you love each other, lying with a man is as natural and spontaneous as breathing. It's a beautiful, wonderful experience,' Mrs Gaskell enthused, and then she giggled. 'But really Charlotte—'

'Laugh all you will, Lily,' Charlotte cut in, affronted. 'I might be gone thirty-eight, but I've not the slightest idea what my role will be.'

'Dear me, Charlotte.'

'What will be expected of me? What I should do? Arthur will probably think me an idiot.'

'Arthur will think nothing of the kind,' Mrs Gaskell reassured her. 'After battling so hard to secure your hand, he'll take great care not to send you running back into the arms of your father,' she said and smiled. 'Perhaps Mr Arthur Bell Nicholls will yet turn out to be the one true love of your life, like the gentleman in your novel, *Villette* – your very own Paul Emanuel; and you, Charlotte, loved and revered by Arthur with a passion to match Paul's love for Lucy Snowe!'

'Professor Paul Emanuel, Arthur Bell Nicholls can never be,' Charlotte said, impassively, adding swiftly and with emphasis when Mrs Gaskell shot a questioning stare toward her. 'But I do love Arthur, Lily, honestly I do, and I possess positive expectations but—'

'In some respects perhaps?' Mrs Gaskell said, askance and furrowing her brow. Charlotte shook her head. 'Reserve judgement until you are married, I say, Charlotte. For once you've sampled life's *real* pleasures you may yet change your mind,' she said and laughed.

Charlotte smiled.

Throughout her stay in Manchester, marriage was

uppermost in Charlotte's mind – marriage was foremost in much of her conversation with Mrs Gaskell. It had been a useful and worthwhile visit, though; Charlotte felt easier about marital duties and expectations. Mrs Gaskell had furnished her with a better understanding of what married life entailed, of what might be expected of her, especially on her wedding night. But after several days Charlotte became impatient to move on; she longed to see Ellen, not least because her friend was crucial to the wedding preparations, and much remained to be done yet.

Tearing herself away from Mrs Gaskell's girls was never easy and on this occasion it was more fraught than usual and Charlotte fought hard to stem her tears: much would pass in the intervening weeks, perhaps months before she next saw any of them. After embracing and kissing each girl in turn, Charlotte's gaze lingered longingly upon the children, Julia especially. Tears blurred her vision, and she convinced Mrs Gaskell that it would be less distressing were she allowed to walk alone to the awaiting carriage and the two friends kissed and said their goodbyes on the doorstep. The coachman collected her luggage and Charlotte, without once turning back, followed him to the awaiting carriage.

It seemed ironic that Mr Gaskell should arrive home as Charlotte was leaving. She had heard his carriage approaching, as she boarded hers. Mr Gaskell was a busy man, and seemed either always arriving home when she was leaving, or going away when she arrived. They waved enthusiastically to each other, but no words passed between them.

However much she enjoyed staying in Manchester with Mrs Gaskell and her family, once the journey to Birstall was underway Charlotte experienced an overwhelming sense of relief. Mrs Gaskell's children had unsettled her; and she could not help thinking that had she married earlier in life, she, too, might have been blessed with a similar happy brood – healthy and boisterous children that might have helped soften the pain of her siblings' passing. But Ellen and her family never failed to settle her nerves.

As had Mrs Gaskell, Ellen, too, became animated the instant she saw the carriage approaching. Racing out from her home and hurrying along the path, stepping up to the coach and pulling the door open before the conveyance had properly stopped. So eager was Ellen to touch again the flesh of her friend, that she almost dragged Charlotte from the carriage, gathering her into her arms before her feet had touched the ground. The pair hugged and kissed and danced like schoolgirls, to the bemusement and amusement of the coachman, who stood watching, scratching his head. He shook his head, and then unloaded Charlotte's luggage and carried it into the house. After receiving his fare, he doffed his cap and wished Charlotte well in her forthcoming marriage, and then left.

Ellen's excitement remained, though, and she practically dragged Charlotte into the living room.

'Look, Mama, Mercy!' she said. 'See how healthy and radiant Charlotte is!'

Mercy spoke first. 'Marriage, it seems, is the cure for all ills,' she said, rising from the sofa and greeting her. 'How well you look, Charlotte.'

'And how thoughtful,' Mrs Nussey began, 'that you should trouble yourself and visit us amidst all the excitement of wedding preparations – all your joy.

'Ellen is fundamental to my wedding preparations, Mrs Nussey; I could scarce hope to be ready in time without Ellen's expert help.'

'Soon to be married…' Mrs Nussey enthused, looking directly at Charlotte, upright and rigid, opening out her fan and fanning her face. 'And to Mr Nicholls… for I believe you had your doubts, Ellen said—'

'Mama!' Ellen cut in. 'Pray do not keep reminding me. I am truly sorry I took the same disagreeable view of Mr Nicholls as Mr Brontë. I was wrong.'

'Well… you and Papa are forgiven, Ellen,' Charlotte said and smiled. 'Indeed, my own first thoughts of Mr Nicholls were not at all favourable. But lasting love, I am reliably informed, grows from nothing and deepens and strengthens with the passing years.'

'I could not have put it better, Charlotte,' Mercy agreed. 'Better than the fickleness of love at first glance – the lustful flash that fizzles out as quickly as it began.'

'Mercy!' Mrs Nussey snapped, lowering her fan onto her lap. 'Take care to avoid using vulgar language.'

'Imagine it,' Mercy continued, ignoring her mother. 'The next time Charlotte visits, it will be as Mrs Nicholls, and she'll have enjoyed more than one fizzing experience, I'm sure…'

'Mercy!' Mrs Nussey again snapped, turning. 'You will visit still, won't you, Charlotte?'

'Of course I'll visit still, Mrs Nussey. I couldn't survive without the good sense and friendship of Ellen – of you all!'

'Well, where marriage suits, there's many that will not,' Mrs Nussey said, adding swiftly. 'Indeed, cannot.'

'I'll not be one of them, Mrs Nussey; I'll be slave to no one,' Charlotte said. 'Ellen and me have been friends since school; we shall always be friends. Life, even after I am married, would be much diminished without Ellen's friendship, without her good sense and advise, without her letters to look forward to.'

Ellen smiled. 'And life without you, Charlotte, would be, well… lifeless.'

'Then may all live long and healthy lives hereafter,' Mrs Nussey said. 'Charlotte especially, when she surrenders her liberty to marriage, to Mr Nicholls.'

'Liberty is not all that Charlotte will be surrendering,' Mercy said and giggled.

'Mercy!' Mrs Nussey admonished, glaring at her daughter. She angled her head upward, picked up her fan and worked it fast, while looking in turn to her daughters, and then to Charlotte, and there her gaze remained.

Chapter Thirty-Two

Mr Nicholls, eager to do the right thing and make a suitable impression, decided to purchase a new suit for the wedding and walked to Keighley. He entered the tailors in ebullient mood and approached the joyless attendant, whose drooping moustache served to accentuate his glum appearance. Nodding tentative acknowledgement, the tailor eyed Mr Nicholls with indifference, and it was not until the curate stated his business that he smiled – an unnatural and exaggerated smile. Wringing his hands in anticipation of profitable business, the tailor procured quickly a selection of fabrics and laid them out on the counter. Mr Nicholls took one look and frowned.

'Something a little less showy, perhaps,' he said and smiled.

'Of course, sir,' the tailor agreed readily. His disappointment, though, was obvious, evident in the petulant manner that he gathered up the samples and took them away. But he looked to Mr Nicholls and forced a smiled. 'It would be unforgivable were you to outshine your bride on her wedding day.'

Procuring a selection of less expensive fabrics, the tailor threw them unceremoniously down on the counter, looking to Mr Nicholls. Smiling excessively, he removed the fraying tape measure from around his neck and took a step closer.

'If I may take a few measurements, while you decide, sir?'

Mr Nicholls nodded. 'Of course.'

The tailor measured Mr Nicholls' neck, and then he took a pencil from behind an ear, licked it and scribbled the measurements down in a notepad. The length of the jacket was measured and recorded, the length of the sleeves, and then the tailor threaded his tape measure through Mr Nicholls' arms and measured his chest, and then his waist, writing the measurements diligently into his notepad, before sinking to his knees before the bemused curate. Mr Nicholls, looking down and frowning, jumped and raised an eyebrow when the tailor pressed one end of the tape measure into his groin. The tailor chuckled and then ran the other end of the tape down to Mr Nicholls' shoe; and then, to the customer's bemusement, he repeated the procedure on his other leg, the attendant's wry grin looking like it might break into laughter at any moment. After struggling back to his feet, trying his utmost to suppress a smile, the tailor recorded the measurements in his notepad and then he looked directly into Mr Nicholls' eyes, clearing his throat.

'On which side does one dress, sir?' he asked, stroking slowly his moustache with a forefinger and thumb, while looking intensely at him.

'I, I beg your pardon,' Mr Nicholls said, eyeing him sternly, and with a puzzled expression.

'Your privates, sir, on which side do they fall?'

'I, I...'

'To the left is the norm, sir, unless—'

'To the left it shall be then, good sir,' Mr Nicholls cut in, smiling confidently.

'Unless John-Thomas is too small to hang, sir, and that would be an *enormous* disappointment to your future bride, wouldn't it?' The tailor said, and then broke into loud outrageous laughter. Unable to curtail his amusement, he turned away and began thumbing distractedly through the fabric samples.

An expression of displeasure contorted Mr Nicholls' features, but he smiled, eventually, if for no other reason than to mollify the tailor's humour. The remaining business was conducted cordially, though, and, after selecting a suitable fabric for his suit, Mr Nicholls chose and purchased a shirt, a tie and a pair of socks. The tailor informed him of the date the suit would be ready to collect, and Mr Nicholls exited the outfitters in a mood that matched his entrance. His smile, though, stretched wider; he was another step nearer in securing Charlotte for his wife.

On returning to Haworth, the curate's exalted mood remained and he smiled readily at the people he met in the village. Many of whom were eager to know the day on which he and Charlotte were to be married. Some, excited greatly upon hearing news of the forthcoming event, wished to be informed of every detail of the wedding. The colour and design of Charlotte's dress, the style of her bonnet and shoes, all of which was more than Mr Nicholls was able to furnish them with.

Everything had been carefully thought through and every detail dealt with or was in hand. Nothing, it seemed, could now stand in the way of Charlotte and Mr Nicholls' marriage.

*

The evening before the wedding was predictably hectic. Ellen had arrived earlier in the day and was with Charlotte in her room, carrying out adjustments to the wedding attire.

After re-stitching a section of hem on Charlotte's dress, Ellen took a pair of scissors, cut the thread and declared the dress almost done and in need of only a few tweaks here and there. She smoothed the white muslin dress with a hand, and then held it up.

'Well, Charlotte, how does it look now?'

Charlotte smiled. 'Very well indeed, Ellen, thank you. Had I attempted the stitching myself I'd have pricked my fingers a thousand times, my eyesight is now so poor.'

Ellen, admiring the dress still, smiled. 'I cannot deny feeling more than a little envious, Charlotte,' she said. 'You'll look beautiful walking down the aisle on the arm of a proud father,' she said and then spread the dress out on the bed.

Charlotte leaned over and began nervously stroking the fabric, when she stopped and turned abruptly.

'Tell me truthfully, Ellen, do you think I do the right thing marrying Arthur?'

'Charlotte!' Ellen exclaimed. 'What thoughts, these? I thought—'

'Marrying Arthur feels right, but at what cost to my liberty. I might never find the time, or space, to write ever again.'

'My dear friend,' Ellen began. 'I can tell by the sparkle in your eyes, by the cheerful disposition that has prevailed since the day you became engaged that marrying Mr Nicholls will suit you well enough. Indeed, it's perhaps the best thing that has happened since… well – and as to your writing, Charlotte. Writing for you is an addiction and addicts will always find the means to feed their habit.'

'Marrying feels right in my heart, Ellen, but—' Charlotte said, halting mid-sentence when a knock resounded on the parsonage door. Negative thoughts were all banished and her face illuminated. 'Miss Wooler! That'll be Miss Wooler,' she said, and then hurried from the room, leaving Ellen drooling over the wedding dress.

Charlotte stepped from the stairs, as Martha opened the parsonage door.

'Miss Wooler.' Charlotte called out, and then skipped across the hall to greet her former teacher. 'How wonderful that you were able to come. I am indeed honoured.'

'How thoughtful that you should invite me, Charlotte,' Miss Wooler said, embracing her, taking her hands, stepping back and scrutinising the bride-to-be. 'My dear Charlotte, it is indeed pleasing to see you looking so well, so happy and so full of life…'

'You are a true friend,' Charlotte said. 'Your presence at my wedding means a great deal to me; and Arthur looks forward to seeing you again.'

Miss Wooler smiled. 'Marriage, Charlotte, the prospect of it, works wonders on you already.'

'My heart is filled with joy. Seldom have I been as happy; not since… well, not since those wonderful days at Roe Head School, learning the rudiments of life under your expert tuition.'

Miss Wooler, distracted by footsteps on the stairs, looked up.

'Ellen, my dear girl! How are you?'

'I'm very well thank you, Miss Wooler,' she said and smiled. 'And it seems the sea air in Hornsea suits you well enough?'

'Indeed it does, but it is the forthcoming joyous event that works its magic on us all,' Miss Wooler said. 'And Margaret, if you please, it's time we dispensed with this Miss Wooler nonsense once and for all. We are equals now. Each of us mature women… so long since teacher and pupil – and Charlotte soon to be married!'

Ellen and Miss Wooler embraced and kissed. Charlotte called to Tabby and asked her to prepare refreshments for herself and her guests and then she shepherded her friends into the dining room. The three ladies sat together and enjoyed refreshments, as they reminisced in some animation over enjoyable past times.

Chapter Thirty-Three

The excitement intensified by the hour and Charlotte, standing motionless in her wedding attire in her room, looked on as Miss Wooler, on her knees on the floor, added a stitch to the dress, while Ellen checked the fit of the dress across Charlotte's shoulders, and then the bride-to-be sneezed. Miss Wooler and Ellen looked to her in horror.

'Oh, no!' Ellen exclaimed. 'How awful to be troubled with the discomfort and inconvenience of a cold on your wedding day.'

'Fret not, Ellen,' Charlotte said, taking a handkerchief to her nose. 'A mere cold is nothing at all, and will quickly be got rid of now that I am happy.'

'Stand still will you, Charlotte,' Miss Wooler bid her. 'Or a cold will not be your only discomfort.'

Laughter followed and then Miss Wooler cut the thread and struggled to her feet. Charlotte took off her dress; Ellen took it from her and arranged on a coat hanger and hung it up while she dressed.

'There…' Charlotte said, straightening her attire. 'That's the last of it now: there's nothing more to be done now until tomorrow.'

The words had barely left Charlotte's lips when a knock, barely audible on the bedroom door, turned the heads of the three ladies. Already ajar, the door was pushed wider to reveal the solemn figure of Mr Brontë, shuffling uneasily on the other side.

'I, I'm sorry, Charlotte, if I… if I throw plans into disarray,' he stuttered, gesticulating uncomfortably. 'But I am unwell and will be unable to attend tomorrow's ceremony.'

'But…' was all that Charlotte could muster. Too shocked to say more, she stood open-mouthed, staring at her father. He, discomfited, turned and walked calmly away.

Ellen and Mrs Wooler looked to each other; they looked to Charlotte and then Ellen pursed her lips and charged from the room.

'Mr Brontë!' she called out. 'You cannot do this. You cannot let your daughter down in this cruel way. Please reconsider.'

'I'm sorry, Ellen,' Mr Brontë said, turning round. 'Truly I am.' And without further explanation, he turned back round and shuffled inside his room and closed the door.

Ellen returned to find Charlotte in tears; tears moistened the eyes of them all, but anger was Ellen's overwhelming emotion. She paced back and forth in the room, until her stoic former schoolteacher, Miss Margaret Wooler, frowning and shaking her head, snatched hold of Ellen's arm.

'Outward outbursts of anger, Ellen, is unbecoming of our sex,' she said, letting go of her arm, and then turning her attention back to the bride-to-be. She pulled out a handkerchief and dried Charlotte's tears. 'Tears are unhelpful also.'

'The wedding will have to be called off,' Charlotte blurted. 'Nothing can be done now at this late hour.'

'Nonsense.' Miss Wooler countered. 'Negativity was not in your vocabulary when you were a schoolgirl. Come, Charlotte, think.' She urged. 'Be as determined as you were in your studies. Where can a man be had at this late hour?

Who do you know who would be willing to give you away? Who would be suitable – acceptable?'

Charlotte composed herself, sniffed; and then inhaled deeply.

'Martha's father, Mr Brown, he...' she offered, but with little enthusiasm, frowning and adding in her next breath. 'Oh, no, John Brown will never do.'

'But does it have to be a man?' Ellen asked.

Miss Wooler looked to Charlotte; and Charlotte and Miss Wooler both turned to Ellen. The ladies shrugged; and then gathered close together, throwing their arms around each other. Speaking at first in whispered tones, but then their discourse grew progressively louder until they spoke with passion, with determined passion.

*

The morning of the wedding was upon them and the two servants, Tabby and Martha were busy, dashing about between the kitchen and dining room. They were vocal and in raptures; buttering bread, slicing joints of meat and making sandwiches, cutting up pies. Plates of sandwiches, pies, buns, biscuits and cakes were carried into the dining room and arranged on the table; jugs of water, fruit cordials, ale and wine were carried in, along with cutlery and plates, mugs and glasses. And then, when Tabby felt that every detail had been attended to, she procured an armful of tea towels and covered over the spread. The servants then removed their aprons to reveal beneath their finest attire and, after smoothing out creases with deft sweeps from practiced hands they were ready, eager to set out for the church. But then Martha began scratching and fidgeting, declaring all of a sudden that practically everything was defective in one way or another; her dress did not fit properly, the sleeves were too long, her petticoat was too tight, this was not right and something else tickled or itched. When one itch had been dealt with Martha discovered, or invented another; and she had no desire at all to wear a bonnet. Tabby insisted, though, and forced one onto her head, but that irritated her ears. Tabby, shaking her head, quickly readjusted her own dress and then glanced at the clock.

'Come, Martha, take my arm.'

Martha obliged and the two servants stepped from the parsonage and, arm in arm, they walked, hobbled, skipped toward the church, thrilled and proud at being witness to their employer, their friend's wedding.

Miss Wooler and Ellen were dressed and ready, but Charlotte was in a fluster. Her dress refused to hang as it should, needing a tweak here and a stitch there, and then she complained that her bonnet was uncomfortable. Miss Wooler removed it, re-positioned it and re-tied the ribbons and the bonnet fit perfectly.

Ellen checked the time.

'We must hurry,' she urged. 'We are ten minutes late already!'

'Poor Arthur,' Charlotte said. 'He's forever hanging about, waiting for me. He'll think I've changed my mind.'

'It'll do him no harm to wait,' Miss Wooler said. 'The longer he is kept waiting, the more appreciative he'll be when you do show up.'

Time, as it is inclined to do when one is in a hurry, passes swiftly and by the time Charlotte and her attendants stepped from the parsonage, they were twenty minutes late.

No one had seen or heard of Mr Brontë all morning and no one, amidst the excitement of the wedding preparations, had thought to enquire after him. All were preoccupied, focussed firmly on their roles. Mr Brontë could have lain dead in his bed and no one would have known.

Chapter Thirty-Four

Guests sitting waiting inside the church, grew increasingly impatient, shuffling constantly on uncomfortable wooden seats, turning their heads with growing anticipation in response to every sound. Some, though, had begun to question whether Charlotte would show up at all. The whisperings sounded louder and grew, and the longer they waited the louder those doubting voices were raised. The officiating minister, standing in front of a nervous groom, checked his watch for the umpteenth time. Frowning and shaking his head, he pushed it back inside his pocket. Mr Nicholls' glanced to him and smiled; it was a nervous smile but, having a better measure of Charlotte's habits, he appeared unduly unconcerned.

The church door creaked open and the minister smiled and shot a hopeful look above the head of the groom; and the people sitting in the pews all turned and smiled. Anticipation, though, was met with disappointment: a latecomer removing his hat, smiling coyly, shuffled into a seat at the rear.

Soon after, the organist, after fingering the same keys over and over, jerking his head and rocking his body to the same dull irritating tune, stiffened and steadied and switched to the music of Mendelssohn's *Wedding March*.

Heads turned and this time, instead of the glum and uncertain looks, widening smiles broke upon the faces of the congregation, and a chorus of sighs greeted the bride. Sighs that mutated rapidly into voluble gasps and stares of bemusement when Charlotte appeared, not on the arm of her father, but on the arm of Miss Wooler. The bride, though, appeared radiant and happy; and her widening, jubilant smile transferred its joy to the faces of those witnessing the occasion.

The wedding ceremony over and done, and the newlyweds emerged from the church; their day blessed with a warm caress, as the sun cast aside its cloudy shroud. Onlookers cheered and whistled and the crowd, prompted by Martha and Tabby, scattered handfuls of confetti and rice over the heads of the joyous couple; and urchins dressed in rags scurried at their feet in search of spilled coins, holding their treasures aloft and grinning upon finding one, regardless of its value.

Charlotte and Arthur, liberated at last from the stresses and uncertainty of the preceding days and weeks, were relaxed and smiling, conversing with the guests, shaking hands, embracing and kissing.

Hunger or thirst dictated the course for an impatient few who stole away, under the watchful if anxious eye of Tabby. The elderly servant, with a despairing stare limped awkwardly after them but desperation struck and her voice boomed as she summoned the services of Martha, imploring her to employ her agile limbs and run on ahead and uncover the spread.

The trickle became a flow, and soon only the bride and groom remained in the churchyard. And they, in no such hurry, were happy to linger; bask in the easy company of each other and enjoy a snatched moment of intimacy on their special day. Clinging to each other they meandered across the soft grass under a tender sun, smiling and kissing, listening to the whispering song of a temperate breeze passing through the long grasses and the trees. Had they not felt it rude or improper they would have fled right then, bypassed the celebratory feast and begun their honeymoon at that magical moment, but to the two attuned hearts, their honeymoon had begun already.

The newlywed's presence at the banquet was eagerly awaited and their entrance stimulated spontaneous applause and cheering. Glasses and cups, charged with wine and ale, were raised; Charlotte and Arthur, once furnished with wine, crossed arms and sipped, smiled and kissed, to a raucous chorus of generous spirited cheering.

Once the adulation had quietened, Charlotte looked anxiously for her father and her face exploded with delight when she spotted him among the guests, conversing and smiling. Charlotte endeavoured to coax a reluctant and nervous husband toward him, succeeding only when Mr Brontë turned his gaze in their direction. Father and daughter embraced, and then father-in-law offered son-in-law a friendly hand.

'Congratulations, Arthur,' he said, gripping his hand, shaking it ardently and smiling. 'Welcome to my family… everyone thinks you and Charlotte make a handsome match – indeed as do I.'

'They are kind, Papa,' Charlotte said, nuzzling her head against his shoulder. 'But the words of others would have been hollow without your blessing,' she said and smiled. 'And I'm glad you felt well enough to leave your sick bed, for I shouldn't have been able to enjoy our honeymoon half as much had you been confined to your bed still, your spirits deflated.'

Mr Brontë smiled. 'And it's good you'll visit Ireland… see the country of my birth,' he said cheerfully, but he sighed deeply with his next breath and adopted a melancholic look. 'But I confess I'll be anxious until you return, Charlotte. For nothing quietens my nerves better than having you around.'

'Well… now that I'm married, you'll likely see more of me,' Charlotte said, turning to her husband. 'Arthur, I'm sure, will not grant me the freedom to gallivant the length and breadth of the country as before.'

'I'll be no tyrant Charlotte, and tie you to the bedpost,' Arthur said, and smiled, somewhat uncomfortably. Mr Brontë frowned and then both men turned when Mr Greenwood approached with an outstretched hand.

'Congratulations, Arthur. You and Mrs Nicholls make a perfect match,' he said, shaking the groom's hand. The stationer's ebullient manner was tempered all of a sudden, and he looked hard at Arthur. 'You'll allow your wife to write still, I trust?'

'Indeed, I shall, Mr Greenwood.'

Charlotte smiled. 'Writing is nourishment to my brain, without it I should wither and die,' she said, turning to her husband. 'And poor, dear Arthur will perhaps wish to have me around a little while longer – I hope.'

'Until you are a hundred, Mrs Nicholls,' Mr Nicholls said and laughed.

Mr Greenwood smiled; he reached out and took hold of Charlotte's hand, lifted it up to his lips and kissed her fingers.

'God bless you, my dear. May you both be happy always, and live long and fruitful lives,' the stationer said and then he let go of Charlotte's hand. He turned, took a glass of wine from the table and raised it in the air. 'Your next novel, Charlotte – and make it a long one,' he said and laughed.

Spontaneous laughter and cheering erupted; Charlotte smiled, but then she became aware of her father's absence.

She looked about and, seeing him select a portion of pie from a plate, Charlotte, smiling wickedly, hastened toward him. And as her father was about to bite into the pie, she snatched hold of his arm and prevented him.

'Papa! No!'

Startled, he turned abruptly.

'Charlotte!'

'Is that wise, Papa?' She said, unsmiling.

'What… to partake of a slice of Tabby's meat pie?'

'But what of the consequences!'

'Consequences…?'

'Might you not suffer excruciating stomach pains?'

'Stomach pains!' he repeated, bemused and frowning.

Charlotte took a step closer and whispered in his ear. 'Has not your back passage closed up?'

Mr Brontë pinched his lips tight together and glared at his daughter, but Charlotte, unable to maintain her stern looks a second longer, burst into loud uproarious laughter, laughter that attracted the attention of everyone in the room and beyond. Mr Nicholls, seeing Mr Brontë's look of outrage, was mortified and he hurried toward father and daughter.

'Is, is something the matter?' He asked, frowning, looking first to his wife, and then nervously to his father-in-law.

Mr Brontë glaring still, turned to Charlotte; and then his features softened and he smiled.

'A private joke, Arthur, nothing more –'

'A joke…'

'And one I couldn't possibly share with you, or with anyone else,' he said, placing a fatherly arm around Charlotte, drawing her closer to him and laughing with her. Arthur laughed, even though he knew not at what but, satisfied that all remained amiable and peaceful, he returned to the guests. Mr Brontë waved the pie in front of Charlotte's face, before biting into it and eating with relish.

Once the plates were all emptied, the ale and wine drunk, the guests began to spill out into the garden, where they milled about in the sunshine, laughing and conversing. Then the steady drumming of horses' hooves prompted the guests to form orderly lines along each side of the garden path. The horses and phaeton stopped outside the garden gate, stirring Martha into action; and she in turn summoned the services of a couple of strong men to help carry the newlywed's trunk to the carriage. The coachman helped the men load it on board, before opening the carriage door in readiness for the bride and groom, and then patiently awaited their presence.

Charlotte and Arthur meandered out from the parsonage, smiling regally, halting on top of the steps when spontaneous cheering and applause rang out and, like a queen with her king, they waved to the admiring hoards. Then they descended the steps and strolled between the lines of appreciative devotees; everyone, it seemed, wished for a word, to shake the hand of the groom, kiss the bride, or all three.

Mr Brontë and Miss Wooler emerged from the parsonage engaged in cordial conversation; they stood side by side and, from the elevated position, they looked out upon the proceedings with justified admiration.

'It's thanks to you, Margaret, that Charlotte, after receiving a first class education, prospers now in her literary endeavours.'

'It's generous of you to say so, Mr Brontë, but Charlotte was an exceptional student, always eager to learn, and teaching her was a pleasure. Charlotte has reaped deserved success; her determination and good sense will, I'm sure, not fail her in marriage either.'

'One prays that it will not,' Mr Brontë said, if somewhat doubtfully.

The bride and groom appeared in no hurry to leave, stopping and chatting, shaking hands and kissing still. Only the coachman, holding the carriage door open, shuffling impatiently, displayed any outward signs of urgency. He cleared his throat noisily.

'The train will not wait in Keighley station forever, ma'am,' he bellowed. 'Famous writer or not.'

Charlotte looked to the coachman and, acknowledging the need for expedience with a curt nod and a smile, tugged at her husband's arm and steered him toward the coach, turning periodically and waving to the appreciative onlookers. Arthur assisted his wife into the carriage and then climbed on board, sitting at Charlotte's side, taking her hands into his and resting them on his lap. The coachman closed the carriage door; he climbed on board and then sat, picked up the reins and called to the horses to walk on. Guests spilled out into the lane and stood waving and cheering until the carriage had disappeared from view along the lane.

Once the guests had all gone Mr Brontë stood alone; a forlorn and thoughtful figure, staring out over the garden. Thinking perhaps, how different it all was when, with his wife and six children, he arrived in Haworth all those years ago. How, after the arduous journey from Thornton, the horses pulling the wagons loaded with their belongings, struggled up the steep road to the isolated hilltop parsonage…

'Are you to stand there with the door wide open all afternoon?'

Tabby's voice bellowed out, rousing him from indulgent thought. Mr Brontë turned round and smiled. Tabby was there still, friend and faithful servant: she had served his family for almost thirty years. Tabby would not desert him; she would be there until the day he breathed his last breath. But for all her dedication and wonderful virtues, Tabby was not family.

Mr Brontë stepped inside and then closed the door.

'Never, Tabby, since leaving Ireland, have I felt so alone,' he said. 'When I first stepped onto English soil, I knew no one. But I was a young man then; it was the beginning of an adventure, an adventure that, from promising beginnings, has been blighted by much tragedy and sorrow. That adventure, I fear, is drawing toward its conclusion – to an unsatisfactory conclusion. I am an old man, and with Charlotte's marriage, I am alone again and with an ageing body that loneliness is felt much keener.'

'But Charlotte won't desert you, Mr Brontë.'

'Charlotte has a husband,' he said, and then shuffled into his study and closed the door. He sank into the chair at his desk, squeezed his hands together and held them over a copy of the bible and closed his eyes.

'Dear Lord, God, watch over my child... please keep my last surviving daughter safe...'

The horses toiled hard, transporting their blissful load up and down the unforgiving hills. The animals, though, were practised; they were strong and made it to the station in Keighley with time to spare, where their efforts were rewarded with a drink of water at a trough, and a bag of oats to restore spent energy and prepare them for their next task.

From the station in Keighley, Charlotte and Arthur caught a train that, after changing several times, delivered them to Conway in Wales. They honeymooned in Bangor until early July, and then boarded the steamer bound for Dublin, Ireland.

Chapter Thirty-Five

The newlyweds enjoyed the first two days of their honeymoon touring Dublin. Arthur proudly showing Charlotte all his favourite places, spending the best part of a day at his former university, Trinity College, where Charlotte claimed she could have spent their entire honeymoon viewing artefacts in the museum and rummaging through the shelves of books in the library. Arthur, though, was eager to move on and introduce Charlotte to his Irish relations.

As had been arranged, Joseph and Mary Anne Bell, Mr Nicholls' cousins, met the honeymooners in the city and transported them to their family home at Banagher: the home where Mr Nicholls was raised by his uncle and aunt. The family home, Cuba House, was a fine mansion set in extensive grounds. Arthur had told Charlotte nothing at all of its splendour, or of the comfortable manner in which her husband's family lived. Nor was she aware of the high regard in which his family were held by the community; and her father's objection to her marrying the 'lowly curate' seemed now risible, and it was Charlotte who felt benefitted most by marriage.

Mrs Bell, having not seen Arthur in years, was overjoyed to be reacquainted with her nephew once again, and that he had brought a bride increased her delight: she embraced and kissed the newlyweds with uninhibited fervour. Widowed some fifteen years earlier, Mrs Bell was the matriarchal head of the family and several of her adult children, Joseph, James, Harriet and Mary Anne, lived with her still. Each was equally thrilled, seeing their cousin again after an absence of many years, and each struggled to believe that Arthur had really married Charlotte Brontë, the famous author of *Jane Eyre*.

Once the honeymooners had freshened up and had changed, Mrs Bell ushered them into the sitting room, where refreshments had been set out. Arthur was hungry after the journey and sat up to the table with his cousins and feasted heartily on pies and sandwiches. Charlotte, though, was tired and ate little; her appetite was compromised by the cold that she suffered still and was content to sit on the sofa next to Mrs Bell, sip tea, nibble on a biscuit and listen to the lively banter flowing from the busy lips of her newly acquired family, and her husband. Her eye, when she could steal it away from Arthur, was drawn from one to the other as each spoke; and she laughed readily at their jokes, even though she had little grasp of Irish humour.

Mrs Bell's eyes, too, were trained upon Arthur for much of the time but she was equally captivated by his bride, and Charlotte secured an equal share of her interest.

'You've made a happy man of our dear boy,' she said, upon observing Arthur conversing and laughing as he ate.

'Arthur has made me happy, Mrs Bell,' she replied, turning to her. 'And it's especially gratifying to be so warmly accepted by you and your family – Arthur speaks well of you all, and I can see why.'

'It's gracious of you to be accepting of us, Charlotte,' Mrs Bell said.

James, who had so far been content to eat rather than speak, cleared his throat and looked to Charlotte.

'Tell me, Miss Brontë, indeed tell all, what are your thoughts so far of Ireland?'

Charlotte turned sharply to him. 'First, may I remind you that Miss Brontë has ceased to exist: I am now Mrs Nicholls,' she affirmed, and then smiled.

'Well said, Charlotte,' applauded Harriet.

James chuckled. 'And your thoughts on Ireland, Mrs Nicholls?'

Charlotte smiled again. 'Since we are now family, is it not better if you address me by my first name, Charlotte?' She said, her smile widening.

'Come, then, *Charlotte*, what of your thoughts of Ireland?'

'Well... I confess to being somewhat biased. Ireland is, after all, the birthplace of my father and affection for the country existed previous to this visit. But from what I have so far seen of the country, Ireland looks a fine place. Indeed, it resembles England in many ways and the people I have met... well, they are very much like English people, so different from what I had been led to believe.'

'Tell us, then, Charlotte, what were you led to believe?' James enquired, looking keenly to her and lifting an eyebrow.

'Well, I, I...' Charlotte stuttered; she blushed and shuffled uncomfortably, realising that she had spoken recklessly and in haste.

'Come, Charlotte, don't be bashful. Tell us, what do you English people say about we Irish?' James demanded, smiling wryly and adding. 'And since we are family, speak plainly, Mrs Nicholls, and spare us the effort of challenging us to translate your slippery English prattle.'

'James!' Mrs Bell remonstrated.

Laughter erupted and Charlotte forced a smile, even though she remained nervous and awkward. After waiting for the laughter to subside, she composed herself.

'Well, please believe me when I say it has never been my

opinion, but many English people think that the Irish are all, well reckless – careless, I suppose, but I…'

Laughter halted her.

'Gormless, is what Charlotte really means,' James interposed, laughing.

'James!' Mrs Bell again admonished.

Charlotte smiled and continued. 'I've so far seen no evidence to suggest that Irish people are any more reckless than the English.'

More laughter erupted and then Mrs Bell turned to Charlotte.

'No, indeed not, Charlotte and I suspect few English people will have ever met an Irish person. I think you'll find it's the nature of the people that matters, that's what determines character, and not the country of one's birth.'

'Indeed,' Mary Anne agreed. 'And Charlotte will know it well enough, I'm sure. She'll have spent many hours studying human behaviour, their peculiarities in order to create the variety of believable characters that feature in her novels.'

'Well, should Charlotte be in any doubt,' Joe began. 'We ungainly Irish folk will endeavour to do all that we can to convince her we can be as civilised as our cultured English cousins.'

Everyone laughed, Charlotte included.

'I can assure you I shall need no convincing,' she said. 'For, before me I see only articulate, warm and friendly people. More capable than many English people that I know.'

'And as skilful, let's hope,' Harriet added, provoking further laughter.

Mrs Bell smiled and looked to Charlotte. 'I can see we are all going to get along very well with Mrs Charlotte Nicholls,' she said.

'Cousin Arthur,' Harriet said, looking to him. 'Don't you think you've made a brave decision in choosing the famous writer, Currer Bell, for your wife?'

'Oh, but Arthur cares nothing at all for the writer, Currer Bell,' Charlotte cut in, 'and says he married only the person, Charlotte Brontë.'

'And quite right, too,' Mrs Bell agreed. 'No one will ever hear Arthur boast that he is the husband of a famous writer.'

'No, indeed not,' Mary Anne concurred. 'Fame and fortune gained by fortunate attachment will not be ill used by our dear cousin, Arthur, I can assure you.'

'Well said, Mary Anne,' Arthur applauded. 'Indeed, I married Charlotte for love and not from any selfish notion of benefiting from her fame, nor for pecuniary gain,' he said and paused. 'But I do confess to one selfish indiscretion and have every intention of showing off Ireland's delights to my beautiful bride, and of boasting unashamedly about every delightful little corner.'

Arthur did just that: the next day he hired a carriage and took Charlotte on a tour of all his favourite places on the island, commenting on them and explaining their finer points with eloquence and enthusiasm – boastfully, it has to be said. The honeymooners rode one day through the Gap of Dunloe on horseback; from there they travelled to Tarbert, a coastal resort situated on the mouth of the Shannon; next Tralee, Bantry Bay and then Cork. It was a whirlwind of indulgent pleasure enjoyed with the restless excitement of persons exploring in a hurry, but the newlyweds were in a hurry. They were determined to see and experience as much of the island's treasures as they were able in the short time that they expected to remain in Ireland on their honeymoon.

Charlotte would have stayed longer had she felt able, but as the weeks passed she became increasingly anxious to see her father again. Despite appearances to the contrary, she knew that he had not been in the best of health when they set out. After dinner one evening, as Charlotte and Arthur walked arm in arm along the sea front in the balmy evening air, they stood together watching the boats bobbing up and down on the swell out at sea, but when Arthur looked next to his bride, the happy face that he had grown accustomed to had been replaced by a melancholic look.

'Charlotte, what—?'

'Oh, nothing, Arthur.'

'You are my wife, Charlotte, when you are sad I am sad also.'

'I was thinking of Papa, that is all, and I wonder how he does.'

'Well, it will not do for my darling wife to worry about her father. Tomorrow we shall pack our bags and prepare to leave this beautiful isle: set sail for England, for home.'

Charlotte tightened her grip around Arthur's waist. 'Dear, Arthur… always so thoughtful and kind,' she said and smiled, and then cast her gaze back out to sea. She stood content and secure in her husband's arms inhaling the warm breeze blowing from the salty ocean, watching the waves racing in, exploding in a crescendo of foaming whiteness on the jagged rocks below. They stood together for some minutes, marvelling at the vastness of the sea, pondering its potential for extraordinary calm or merciless violence. Charlotte smiled and nuzzled her head against Arthur's shoulder.

'True love…' She uttered. 'So much better than foolish obsession.'

'Foolish obsession!' Arthur repeated, looking sternly to her.

'Juvenile crushes… are we not all at some point in our lives guilty of some such futile indiscretion? Imagined love with a fantasy lover that can never become reality?' She lifted her head from Arthur's shoulder, and looked into his eyes.

'Well, Charlotte,' he began, gazing lovingly upon her. 'My foolish obsession is indeed real: my fantasy love has turned into this marvellous reality and yet it all seems like a wonderful, improbable dream.'

They laughed, they kissed, they hugged and then kissed some more.

'Oh, Arthur, I wish our honeymoon could last forever.'

'It will, dear wife, it will… long after we have forsaken this beautiful island and are back at home in England,' he said, drawing Charlotte tighter to him. 'Our life together, I promise, will be one long honeymoon.'

Charlotte was extraordinarily happy and she could hardly believe that in Arthur she had found such a caring, considerate man whose own needs seemed always secondary to hers. That he should care about her father, and especially after all that had been said, increased her happiness. Her father was all that remained of the once large, happy and spirited family.

Mr Brontë was an old man, though, and would not live forever. He had reached an age when rising from one's bed of a morning was reason enough to rejoice. For how often, in those declining twilight years, does a peaceful night's sleep light up the glittering pathway? The path that leads to the mystical kingdom, the palace of rest we all dread but where we will one day dwell, for the reservation has already been made.

Chapter Thirty-Six

Martha, swinging the carpet beater, grimaced and grunted each time the elaborately patterned wicker instrument struck the carpet hanging over the washing line in the garden. The day was scorching hot and the afternoon sun seemed stuck in the sky directly overhead, beaming its oppressive heat upon the young servant. She was irritable and appeared angry, resting periodically, nipping her lips tight together and wiping her brow, before gripping the carpet beater between both hands and swinging her shoulders round and attacking the carpet like it had done her an injustice; and harm had been inflicted: the physical exertion made her arms and back ache, the dust stung her eyes and it made her cough.

She halted again and wiped her brow; she coughed and spat, and then as she repositioned her feet in readiness to strike the carpet again, the clatter of horses' hooves and the voice of the driver calling to the animals to steady, provided reason to prolong her rest. She looked up and toward the lane. Horses and then a carriage came into view and Martha's face lit up. She threw the carpet beater down on the grass and raced inside the parsonage.

'Charlotte's back! Charlotte… Mr and Mrs Nicholls are home,' she shouted as she charged through the hall and into the dining room, where Tabby, her eyes closed, rested in a chair. 'Tabby, Tabby, wake up!' She bellowed, shaking the elderly servant.

'What the!' Startled and disorientated, the elderly servant opened her eyes, her arms flailing wildly about. 'Get from me, get…' she yelled; and then she saw Martha. 'Charging about like a lunatic… frightening the life from me! You'll bring about a seizure and have me in my grave before you're done.'

'Miss Brontë's back, Miss Bronte's back home, Tabby.'

'It's Mrs Nicholls now, I'll have you know,' Tabby reminded her. 'And you'll have Mr Nicholls to answer to should you forget it.'

Martha shrugged; she took hold of Tabby's arm and helped hoist her up out of her chair and onto her feet; and then she charged from the room toward Mr Brontë's study and thumped on the door.

'Mr Brontë, Mr Brontë! Charlotte's—' she shouted, lurching back when the door opened.

'Yes, yes, Martha – I've this minute watched Charlotte climb down from the carriage.'

'It's Mrs Nicholls now, Mr Brontë,' Martha said. 'And you'll know about it if you forget.'

'Yes, yes, all right,' he said, shaking his head as he shuffled into the hall.

Tabby returned to the kitchen and lifted a couple of mugs down from a shelf and set them on the table. She picked up the milk jug, sniffed at it, scowled and recoiled but then from a rusting metal churn, she added more milk to the jug, sniffed it again, smiled and then poured a small amount of milk into each mug.

Martha raced outside and along the garden path and Charlotte, hearing the patter of footsteps and the servant's excitable voice, turned round.

'Everyone thought you were never coming home,' Martha said. 'Thought you might stay in Ireland forever.'

'Well, we are home,' Charlotte said and smiled, and then embraced the servant. 'It's good that you are well, Martha, but tell me, how is Papa?'

'Well enough, I dare say,' Martha said, as she stood scrutinising Charlotte. 'And your cold, it's—?'

'Cured. Yes, Martha,' Charlotte cut in, beaming. 'Arthur and his wonderful family took good care of me in Ireland,' she said, cuddling up to her husband.

The coachman lifted the trunk from the carriage and set it down on the ground. Martha took one end, he the other and they set off along the garden path with it.

Mr Brontë appeared on the steps and Charlotte, impatient to feel her father's flesh pressed against hers once again, wriggled free from her husband and ran up the steps to greet him. Father and daughter hugged and kissed like they had they been separated for years. Arthur paid the coachman and then joined his wife and father-in-law. Mr Brontë extended a hand.

'Welcome home, Arthur,' he said, taking his son-in-law's hand and shaking it vigorously. 'Ireland, it seems, has done you both good,' he said, looking from him to Charlotte and back. 'And did you take Charlotte to the Loughbrickland district, to Emdale – the place where I was born?'

'I dare not leave Ireland without.'

As they meandered inside, their spirited voices drew Tabby out from the kitchen and into the doorway, where she stood, wiping her hands on her pinafore, casting a scrutinising eye over the newlyweds.

'You both look half starved,' Tabby cried. 'Has neither eaten since the day you left Haworth?'

'Of course we have, Tabby,' Charlotte said, looking to her husband, smiling. 'Arthur's family were indeed both accommodating and generous, but Arthur and me had interests other than eating to occupy our time, didn't we, Arthur?'

'Aye, I dare say you had,' Tabby said, chuckling knowingly.

'Travelling around Ireland, is what Charlotte meant,' Arthur was quick to add, flashing an uneasy glance toward Mr Brontë. 'Taking in the sights... visiting my relations – of which there are many.'

'I've sliced some ham,' Tabby said, returning to the kitchen. 'And the kettle's about boiling.'

Food was served on the table in the dining room, but Charlotte, after the tiring journey, had little appetite. Sitting dutifully at the side of her husband; she took a sip of coffee, scowled, glanced at Tabby and then shook her head, but she continued to drink the beverage. She sat and watched as Arthur tucked heartily into the plate of ham, cheese, bread and butter; and as the food on Arthur's plate diminished, Charlotte transferred the ham and cheese from the plate in front of her onto her husband's. When Arthur had eaten to his fill – consuming all the food from both plates – he took Charlotte's hand in his, raised it up to his lips and kissed her fingers and then enveloped both her hands in his and rested them upon his lap.

Mr Brontë, sitting by the fire, scanning the pages of a newspaper through the magnifying glass he held, glanced periodically to them and smiled. Their eyes met and smiles lit up the faces of them all, warm and generous smiles. Peace prevailed, it seemed, and passions were all calmed.

Chapter Thirty-Seven

Arthur and Charlotte joined Mr Brontë by the fire. After watching them sit, the ageing parson allowed the newspaper to fall onto his lap and then he began to inform them of events having taken place in the parish during their absence. Much was pertinent to the church, or to issues concerning public health, which tested Charlotte's ability to remain awake. After only a short time she rested her head on her husband's shoulder and then closed her eyes. Arthur noticing, smiled; he looked lovingly upon her and then turned back to Mr Brontë, and the two men proceeded to discuss a number of issues in some detail.

Minutes later, after Mr Brontë had picked up the newspaper, Arthur seized his opportunity. Yawning exaggeratedly, he turned and put his lips to Charlotte's ear and whispered. Her eyelids flipped open instantly and she appeared momentarily stunned, but a smile broke slowly upon her lips and she lifted her head from Arthur's shoulder. She stood up, took hold of her husband's hands and helped haul him to his feet. Mr Brontë looked to them.

'You'll both be tired after your journey, I expect,' he said. 'Be ready for a good night's sleep.'

'Eventually,' Charlotte quipped, looking to Arthur and smiling.

Arthur reciprocated, if with a muted smile.

Mr Brontë looked severely to them; he cleared his throat and then shook the newspaper.

'Well, goodnight,' he said, lowering his head and focussing the magnifying glass over a page.

'Goodnight, Papa,' Charlotte said, as she steered her husband toward the door.

'Goodnight, Mr Brontë,' Arthur said, turning briefly to him, before whispering again in Charlotte's ear. When she giggled, Mr Bronte looked sternly to them, shaking the newspaper more aggressively that before, as if in in a statement of disapproval.

Mr and Mrs Nicholls lay on their backs in bed beneath the covers, motionless and silent. The fitful light from a candle, set on a bedside cabinet next to Arthur, danced playfully upon their faces. The romance of its stuttering light, though, was compromised by the intrusive constancy of the moonlight shining inside through the un-shuttered windows.

Arthur smiled and turned expectantly to Charlotte.

'Shall I snuff out the candle?'

'Let it burn a while longer, Arthur,' Charlotte said, snuggling tighter to him and gazing lovingly into his eyes.

Unable to hide his disappointment completely, Arthur smiled; and he leaned over and kissed his wife's forehead.

'I feel the happiest man in England,' he said. 'Nay, the entire world.'

'To me, it seems a dream I will one day rudely awaken from,' Charlotte said, smiling distractedly. And then her smile disappeared all of a sudden and she turned abruptly to her husband. 'You will keep your promise, though, won't you, Arthur?'

'For as long as your father draws breath, darling wife.'

Charlotte's smile widened, and she cuddled tighter to

her husband. 'My only concern now is that with you to care for I'll find little time for writing.'

'Don't you feel you've written enough, Charlotte?'

'No, Arthur!' She responded, mortified by the suggestion, and by the austere tone of his voice. She released him, rose up over him and glared. 'Never, not since my sisters and Branwell wrote poetry together have I stopped writing. You'll not make me, will you?'

'No, no…' Arthur replied, chuckling and pulling her gently back to him. 'Of course not, dear wife. I'll be no tyrant, Charlotte. If writing is what makes you happy, who am I to dictate what you can and cannot do?'

'You are my husband, Arthur… I promised to obey.'

'Well…' Arthur uttered dismissively, shaking his head and smiling.

Charlotte snuggled back up to him; she leaned over and kissed his cheek, and then his lips, again and again until their kisses merged into one. Arthur, breathing exaltedly, rose up and rolled her over onto her back and lowered himself onto her and began kissing her with increasing passion. Charlotte, struggling to catch her breath, stopped his kisses.

'You may snuff out the candle now, Arthur,' she said and smiled.

Arthur licked a forefinger and thumb and quickly nipped out the flame and then he and Charlotte slipped lower beneath the sheets, watched over by the glare of a fretful moon. Hands fumbled and nightgowns were loosened and hitched up. Lips feasted on lips and lips feasted on flesh, and moans, hushed and breathy, burgeoned and became increasingly piercing and tuneful; the bed squeaked and the floorboards creaked.

Sitting by the fire in the dining room, Mr Brontë was irritable and unable to concentrate on the newspaper he held. Tightening his lips; he glanced periodically and with disapproval up to the ceiling, shaking his head and frowning. He cleared his throat and rustled the pages of newspaper; he tried everything he could to blot out sound of the amorous newlyweds in the room above. A look of horror contorted his face when Tabby, carrying a tray with warm milk and oat biscuits, hobbled into the dining room. Chuckling and grinning, she set the tray down on the table and then looked directly into the eyes of the tormented parson, motioning with a knowing, upward nod of her head.

'There'll be children running about the parsonage before long, Mr Brontë… the sour smell of nappies.'

'God forbid!' He returned, aghast and with eyes widening. He picked up a biscuit, bit into it and chewed, while eyeing Tabby with a deep furrowed brow.

'God forbid!' Tabby repeated slowly. 'Why, Mr Brontë, children running about the parsonage would take ten years of us both,' she said, casting her gaze upward once again. 'The good Lord will decide, not you or I—'

'The good Lord!' Mr Brontë barked. 'I wish to God the good Lord would open up the roof and rain icy water on those rutting—'

'Mr Brontë!' Tabby, interrupting, shrieked. She stood a moment, chuckling and shaking her head, angling her head and listening. 'It'll take more than icy water to cool their ardour,' she said and then limped away, chuckling.

The moans heightened and the floorboards rattled, creaking and squeaking until achieving a steady rhythm, a rhythm that increased until reaching a disorientating climax that screamed its torment inside Mr Brontë's head. The newspaper fell onto his lap and, while staring straight ahead, he listened until he could stand no more and then he let go of the magnifying glass and cast the newspaper from his lap and clamped his hands over his ears. But Charlotte's cries, her euphoric screams, echoed alarmingly inside his head long after the room above had fallen silent.

Chapter Thirty-Eight

Arthur kept his promise, and Charlotte continued to write. Additional to the novels, she wrote copious letters to friends, Ellen Nussey especially.

"Dearest Nell,

I hope you and your family are well, as we in Haworth all are. My dear boy flourishes like you would not believe. Arthur is especially healthy and busy; he is strong and attentive... Many people had misgivings, but marrying Arthur is the best thing I have done in an age. Indeed, married life suits better than I could have ever imagined. Life is one long whirl of pleasure and contentment. The nastiness is all in the past, and Arthur and Papa get along marvellously..."

Charlotte smiled and looked toward the door when the sound of approaching footsteps distracted her. The door creaked open and the footsteps stopped and Arthur appeared in the doorway, smiling. His eye shot straight to the letter that she was writing, and his smile was replaced by an anguished glare.

'Not more letters, Charlotte!' He decried, shuffling closer and looking over her shoulder.

'Only to Ellen, Arthur.'

His hand rested gently upon her shoulder and he leaned over her and read the letter she was writing. Charlotte, feeling her husband's warm breaths upon her neck, smiled and, without turning, lifted up a hand. She found his arm and stroked it.

'I trust Ellen destroys your letters once she has read them?'

Exasperated, Charlotte let go of his arm and turned round sharply.

'I know not what Ellen does with my letters. I do not ask her.'

'Then you must, Charlotte. You must instruct Ellen to destroy your letters once she has read them… insist that she burns every trace of them.'

'No, Arthur, I cannot. Once I have sent the letters they are Ellen's to do with them as she pleases.'

'You are a famous writer, Charlotte,' Arthur stressed. 'Your letters are of interest to the public and should they one day fall into the wrong hands, they may be put to unscrupulous use.' He paused, and then sighed. 'Please say you'll do as I ask, dear wife.'

'But, Arthur—'

'If you will not do as I ask or if Ellen refuses to destroy your letters – every last trace of them – you must write no more details of our private life.'

'But Arthur—'

'No buts, Charlotte.'

'Very well,' she grudgingly conceded, nipping her lips tight together and turning abruptly from him. 'You are my husband, and I *will* obey, even though your demands are utterly detestable to me.'

Arthur smiled uncomfortably; he leaned over and kissed his wife's cheek.

'Pray do not think this an act of tyranny, Charlotte. I do it solely for your own good, dearest wife.'

'Yes, yes, Arthur,' Charlotte said, sighing resignedly.

She turned to him and smiled and then her demeanour brightened. 'If you are going out again, walk not far, Arthur, for the wind remains bitter yet – I fear we'll have snow soon.'

'Worry not, dear wife, Anne's old dog will see that I do not venture far. He abhors the cold these days,' Arthur said. He hovered over her for some more minutes, observing Charlotte as she wrote, before stealing quietly away, halting and standing a while longer and watching from the dining room doorway.

Charlotte, sensing that his presence remained, completed the sentence she was writing and then turned, but Arthur had gone. She smiled, sat and listened for the clash of the parsonage door closing; and then her smile widened and she wrote:

"…You'll laugh when I tell you, Ellen, but Arthur has this minute instructed me to insist that you burn my letters once you have read them. I demand no such action, of course, should you wish to keep them. The letters are yours once they are in your hands and I care not what you do with them, but please say you'll destroy the letters when you next write. It will put Arthur's mind at ease and our friendship can continue as before…"

Marriage had transformed Charlotte's life: she was content and happy; gone were the headaches that blighted her days and kept her awake at night. Life had meaning, it had purpose and in Arthur she had found a caring and loving husband: a worthy distraction from the lonely hours spent writing. Since marrying, creativity was no longer the sole therapeutic activity that helped thwart the rumblings imposed by tragedy. Charlotte had a man to love and care for; she had a man to return that love and care. She was happy and content, achieving in marriage a fulfilled state that was unattainable living a singular life.

Life, though, is an unending trial; a constant battle against a barrage of random events, all conspiring to end life. That one exists at all is a testament to remarkable luck, to an improbable sequence of events, without which life would be impossible. Life is the one true miracle of this world.

Fleeting pleasures are few and are presented to us in order to be seized upon and enjoyed. For all too often, sometimes after an extended period of suffering when some semblance of happy normality returns, from innocuous beginnings events take hold that darken that light, setting in motion a train of events, an unstoppable spiral of decline that gains a determined momentum of its own, which no amount of loving care or prayers can arrest.

Chapter Thirty-Nine

The winter of eighteen fifty-four was cold and unforgiving, as indeed were many winters in nineteenth century England. Snow fell upon Haworth and the surrounding moors in early November and the harsh frosts turned the snow to ice, inconveniencing life even further. It was a brutal and bitter month and respite from the cruel winter weather arrived only with the final week of November. A thaw set in that melted much of the snow, leaving behind only grimy remnants: stubborn, angled drifts that rested against the limestone walls and fences where the snow had lain the deepest. With the milder days, though, came the rain and restless broody skies that hid away the sun. Daylight hours, already scarce, were shortened further by the ominous dark shadow of heaven.

The days were dreary and endless, cold and wet, and Charlotte remained shut inside the parsonage for much of the month, sitting huddled by the fire, working on her new novel, *Emma*. Then one day a glimmer of vivid orange light shining inside through the window dazzled and distracted her. Charlotte put aside her work, stood up and walked to the window and looked out upon the first meaningful sight of the sun in weeks. She longed to step out under its rays, feel its warming rays again upon flesh and bones that ached from siting too long in cold, damp rooms. But it remained cold still; it was cold inside and estrangement from the fire provoked a shiver, prompting a swift return to the fireside. After warming her hands, she sat down, picked up her pen and wrote several sentences quickly and neatly, pausing at intervals, and then writing some more; and soon another paragraph had been completed, and then another chapter. She rested awhile, composing mentally the opening sentences of a new chapter, when a plume of smoke billowed out from the fire. The outer door had been opened, Charlotte knew and she smiled and looked toward the dining room door and listened. Her smile widened upon hearing the rustle of clothing and scuffed footsteps in the hall.

'Is that you, Arthur?' She called out, and then wrote down quickly the opening sentences of a new chapter.

The expected reply failed to arrive but, conscious of the dining room door being opened, Charlotte looked to it; her smile widened yet further when Arthur shuffled into the doorway.

'Busy with another—'

'Is it cold out still, Arthur?'

'It's a little warmer than of late, now most of the snow has melted,' he said. 'Breezy yet, but, but…' he halted mid-sentence and took a step closer as his eyes homed in on Charlotte's writing, and then his tone hardened. 'Another letter to Ellen!'

'No, Arthur… *Emma.*'

'Emma?'

'My new novel.'

'Ah… I see,' he said and paused, his features brightening. 'But there's no need to tire yourself out with work, Charlotte. We have money enough to meet our present needs – I earn, too, don't forget.'

'Yes, Arthur, I know you do. But once the germ of a story forms inside my head it almost writes itself. All I have to do is to hold my pen to the page – transfer the energy from my brain to paper before my head explodes. And the extra money will be useful especially if—'

'Well… we'll have to wait and see.'

Several more sentences slipped fluently from Charlotte's pen and she, conscious of her husband's lingering presence, glanced periodically to him, stopping completely only once the first paragraph of the new chapter had been drafted. She looked to him, smiling warmly.

'Well… have you taken to wearing your coat inside now, Arthur?'

'No, no, I thought I might take a short walk.'

Charlotte dipped her pen in the inkwell and was about to write some more, but she hesitated upon noticing his continued imploring stare.

'Ah, I see, you wish me to accompany you?'

'If… only if you can bear to be parted from *Emma*,' he said and then smiled.

'To where did you intend walking?'

'I thought the waterfall… flushed with the melted snow. But, no, the waterfall is perhaps too far for an uncertain November afternoon.'

'It sounds a splendid idea to me,' Charlotte said. 'The clouds have begun to break apart and disperse, and I've already seen the sun. Perhaps it will oblige us and accompany us to the waterfall and back?' She put down her pen and gathered the pages of her manuscript together, set them aside and then stood up. '*Emma* will have to be patient.'

The sun did shine, if only intermittently, but when it shone it was warm and pleasant and enhanced the pleasure of walking over the exposed moorland to the waterfall on that November afternoon. Flossy, Anne's ageing spaniel, accompanied them. Sniffing inquisitively about the dry stalks of heather, barking at the rabbits whenever one emerged from hiding and chanced its luck. The rabbits, though, had nothing to fear; barking was as much as the old dog was now able to threaten.

After walking for an hour or more, the clouds began to gather and thicken; the wind blew stronger and colder, and by the time they reached the waterfall, the clouds had swallowed up the sun completely. Arthur, standing behind Charlotte, held her tight in his arms and together they looked with wonder at the frothing white torrents cascading down over the rocks, churning angrily in the stream below and rushing away.

Arthur was uneasy, though, looking periodically up to the sky; anxiously at the black clouds that hovered ominously above the rocky outcrop, threatening to release their burdensome moisture. He thrust out a hand.

'Rain is in the air, Charlotte! We must return home at once,' he urged, letting go of her.

Charlotte turned sharply to him. 'But we've only this minute arrived, Arthur! Let's stay a while longer and enjoy the watery spectacle while we are able. We may never again witness the waterfall in its winter fury.'

'To delay, I fear, is folly, Charlotte, but, if it pleases you…'

'Worry not, dear Arthur,' Charlotte said, taking his arm and smiling, looking up at the clouds. 'Any rain will pass quickly.'

The rain fell light at first but before long, raindrops the size of small pebbles splashed down upon them, drenching them in little time. Arthur removed his coat and held it over Charlotte's shoulders, but it was too late, she was already soaked as he hurried her toward some overhanging rocks. The shelter there proved inadequate and rain dripped upon them from the cold grey rocks, rocks that had turned a darker shade in the rain, but nor did the rain pass quickly.

Arthur, agitated and distraught, stepped out from beneath the shelter and looked up to the sky.

'Arthur… step back under the rocks, dear boy, and relax,' Charlotte bid him, reaching out, taking hold of his arm and coaxing him back under the shelter. 'Let not a shower of rain ruin our pleasure.' She smiled and then pointed. 'Look, see, the blackest clouds have passed over us already.'

The darkest clouds had passed on, but the rain fell still and the pair stood huddled together shivering, waiting, hoping and praying that the rain would stop soon.

When a meaningful break in the clouds did eventually appear, Arthur sighed and Charlotte smiled. The clouds thinned and parted and the sun glided majestically into the widening fissure. Its dazzling light illuminating the saturated moorland, transforming insipid pools into sparkling jewels.

Arthur and Charlotte stepped out from beneath the rocks and he, holding the coat over his wife's shoulders, hurried her homeward. The coat was wet and cold, it was heavy and uncomfortable and the hem flapped angrily in the wind but worse, Charlotte's feet shod in flimsy fabric shoes were frozen, submerging beneath the cold, dark pools with every foot falling onto the sodden heathland. Only Flossy, muddied and bedraggled, appeared to gain any pleasure from the frenetic homeward dash, barking and dancing about their legs, splattering them with muddy water.

They had not long set out from the waterfall when the wind strengthened, and ugly black clouds crept back overhead and swallowed up the sun. The pair ran with greater urgency, but were unable to outrun the storm clouds. Rain and hail, heavy and persistent fell upon them, soaking and battering them in the gusting wind. All they could do at times to secure some measure of respite from the storm was to stop and turn their backs to the onslaught and wait for the worst to pass.

Mr Brontë, sitting at his desk in his study, looked to the window and at the rain and hail hammering against the glass panes. He stood up and stepped to the window and looked out; smiling and looking with wonder upon the dense torrents chasing one another across the hillside. A knock on the door startled him; and it awakened a thought.

'Is Charlotte home, Tabby?' He asked, frowning as he turned to her.

'She's not,' Tabby snapped, shaking her head, nipping her lips together. She set the mug and biscuits she carried down on his desk. 'Charlotte and her husband set out for the waterfall hours ago.'

'The waterfall! But, but… the fools!' He retorted, shuffling away from the window and sitting down at his desk. He picked up the mug of coffee, but put it back down without tasting it, taking a biscuit instead and biting into it. Chewing ardently while focussing upon the rain-lashed windows, staring distractedly and shaking his head.

The parsonage came into view and, as if by some perverse godly act, the rain stopped and the sun broke through the fragmenting clouds. Charlotte and Arthur, soaked and cold and breathless, halted: she looked up to the sky, and then faced her husband, smiling smugly.

'I said any rain would soon pass, didn't I, Arthur?' She boasted and then laughed.

'Make not light of a foolish situation, Charlotte,' Arthur snapped, turning sharply to her and glaring. 'Your father will be furious.'

'But, Arthur, we are almost ho- ho-... a-a-a-choo.'

Arthur's glare morphed rapidly into one of concern and each time Charlotte sneezed, he winced. He pulled a handkerchief out from his pocket, wrung the water from it and then handed it to his wife.

'Why Charlotte, why! Why did I drag you away from your writing? Encourage you to leave our warm dry home and walk on the moors – walk all that distance to the waterfall in the middle of winter!'

'Calm your temper, dear husband,' Charlotte bid him, taking his arm and drawing him to her side. 'We are almost home.'

Home, though, was not the welcoming haven they might ordinarily have expected it to be. The instant Charlotte and Arthur stepped inside the parsonage they were met, not with sympathy, but with the combined wrath of Mr Brontë and Tabby. Tabby attacked first.

'Fools!' She shrieked. 'What in heaven's name were you both thinking? Look at you: wet through and shivering!'

Charlotte sneezed.

'You should know better, Charlotte,' Mr Brontë retorted; he was outraged and glared unsympathetically at her as she continued sneezing. 'Damn it, you do know better than to traipse about the cold, wet moors in winter. You know your constitution is not robust, yet you—'

'Take a shovel next time and dig your graves—' Tabby cut in.

'Next time!' Mr Brontë interrupted. 'There'll be no next time.'

'My fault entirely,' confessed Arthur.

'Nonsense,' Charlotte countered. 'Had I not wished to walk to the waterfall I would have said so and not gone. I am your wife, Arthur, not a caged bird let out to sing only when granted permission.'

'Were you a bird I'd break your wings,' snapped Tabby. 'Put a stop to your foolishness wandering,' she continued, thrusting an armful of clothes toward Charlotte. 'Here… get out of your wet clothes and change into these before you catch your deaths.'

'Thank you, Tabby,' Charlotte said curtly, forcing a smile and snatching the garments from her and then hurrying upstairs with them. Arthur scurried after her.

'There'll be mugs of beef tea waiting when you're done,' Tabby shouted after them.

Arthur turned back and smiled. 'Thank you, Tabby.'

Out of earshot, Charlotte and Arthur turned to each other and giggled, disrespectfully, like scolded schoolchildren escaping the wrath of an authoritarian master. Attempting to enter their bedroom together, they each impeded the other and their laughter heightened. Arthur gesticulated and gave way to his wife, resting his hands on her hips and hurrying her inside. The instant he closed the door they began tearing at each other's clothing, kissing and giggling, caressing and stroking each other's cold-wet flesh. Seconds later they were naked. Charlotte threw back the bedsheets and she and Arthur leapt onto the bed, pulling the sheets up over them. Indulging immediately with the urgency of bodies greedy for warmth, greedy for each other.

Chapter Forty

Tabby's beef tea, for all its supposed nourishing, health-giving properties could neither ward off illness nor arrest the unseen malice working its evil inside Charlotte's frail body. Arthur blamed himself for her ill health, brought about, he felt certain, after encouraging her to walk the considerable distance to waterfall on that cold and wet November afternoon.

Each time Charlotte coughed, sneezed or wheezed, if he heard a groan or a sniffle, he stopped whatever he was doing and rushed to her bedside. Once there, he knelt on the floor beside her bed and held her hand and through doleful eyes he gazed longingly upon her; he stroked her forehead and attempted to soothe her with soft-spoken words. When she slept he watched over her, fretting over every insignificant twitch or groan.

'Fool! I should have left you in peace to write your novel,' he chuntered, 'instead of dragging you outside in the middle of winter to walk the wet and windswept moors. Damn it, I should have had more sense, taken better care of my precious, darling wife—'

'Pray, Arthur, please stop it!'

'Well, I should at least have provided you with an overcoat that would have kept you dry. Damn it, why?'

'Arthur! If you do not moderate your language, you're likely to suffer a far worse fate than me… be struck down by some incurable affliction that makes my suffering seem nothing at all.'

'Well… I should have let you alone to write your novel.'

'Do stop blaming yourself, Arthur and go. For heaven's sake let me alone and go to your parishioners.'

'I'll fetch the doctor first… have him come and examine you.'

'Arthur… I am in need of no doctor,' she stressed, reaching out and taking hold of his arm, stroking it and smiling. 'Your love is medicine enough; your love and Tabby's beef tea. So please go, Arthur; go and discharge your duties to your parishioners and when you return you may bestow all the pampering you wish.'

Charlotte's illness remained stubborn: the doctor was called, but the medicines he prescribed invariably made her worse. The days of suffering turned into weeks, and her health continued to deteriorate; and as the weeks turned into months her body began to weaken and her suffering became progressively worse. She was sick of a morning, her appetite was poor and it mattered not whether she lay in bed all day, or if she sat by the fire in the dining room, Charlotte was able to obtain no relief. She was irritable, in pain and uncomfortable for much of the time, and the headaches and sickness that marriage had tamed returned with a vengeance; and the peaceful night's sleep that she had begun to enjoy, safe and warm, enveloped in her husband's strong arms, was no more.

Sitting in her chair by the fire one day, Charlotte endeavoured to take her mind off her plight and write another chapter of *Emma*. But the effort required in order to make a start drained her completely but she took up her pen nevertheless, and a sheet of paper and wrote. But after scribbling down only a few disjointed lines, her brain protested and it became impossible to compose a coherent sentence. The one-time enjoyable pleasure of plotting the next line, the next paragraph, proved impossible to achieve with a mind distracted by pain; with a malnourished body depleted of energy and utilising every ounce of strength in a desperate fight for survival. She was hot one minute and cold the next. If she moved closer to the fire, she felt flushed and feverish; and when she shuffled her chair back she shivered. When she could sustain her concentration no longer, in a fit of frustration she threw *Emma* aside and snatched a sheet of writing paper from her desk.

"Dearest Ellen,

I trust you are in better health, and in a better frame of mind, than I currently am. Headaches have not left me in weeks. I am sick most mornings and am unable to do the things that have given me most pleasure – writing, and latterly satisfying Arthur's needs. It was kind that you should invite me to stay; and I should very much like to see you, but while I remain unwell my husband will not permit me to travel. The journey, he says, will tire me and make my illness worse. He is my husband…"

Mercy collected the mail from the postman and hurried into the living room with it, handing Ellen the letter addressed to her. Ellen glanced at the handwriting on the envelope and smiled: she had not heard from Charlotte in over a fortnight.

Sitting on the sofa next to her mother, Ellen tore open the envelope. She removed the letter from the envelope and opened it out and her smile slowly vanished.

'What is it, Ellen?' Mrs Nussey said, noticing, calmly cooling her face with her fan. 'What does Charlotte say?'

Ellen's head moved from side to side as she consumed

the words. 'What Charlotte says, Mama, I cannot tell, the words are not hers. Nicholls dictates to her, I'm sure; and he refuses to let Charlotte visit while she remains unwell and he will not let me visit Charlotte.' Ellen spat, her mouth twisting with contempt. 'Nicholls, that wretched husband bullies her. *He* says what she can write, *he* says what she can and cannot do. That man, Mama, that awful man she married—'

'Calm your temper, Ellen, dear,' her mother demanded, stroking her arm. 'Dear me, and I thought your hostilities toward Mr Nicholls had ended?'

'Well, they are reversed, Mama,' snapped Ellen. 'Nicholls… first he made a liar of me. Forcing me to make promises I could not, and would not keep. And then he forced Charlotte to walk with him on the moors in the rain in the middle of winter.' Her voice faltered and turned tremulous. 'Poor, Charlotte… she's been unwell ever since that day, and now that awful man she married prevents her from visiting until she is better. Charlotte will not get better, Mama, if Nicholls is determined to keep her locked up in a cage and prevented from singing – denied the freedom she has enjoyed and been used to ever since she was a child.'

'Mr Nicholls is Charlotte's husband, Ellen. He loves her and wants only what's best for her,' Mrs Nussey said. 'It's a husband's duty to nurse his wife – *to love and to cherish in sickness and in health* – he agreed to it in his marriage vows, he spoke it in God's residence for all to hear. It's Mr Nicholls' duty to care for her, and Charlotte doesn't complain, does she?'

'Charlotte's not allowed to complain. Nicholls vets her letters, and she is able to write only what he dictates.' Ellen lifted the letter closer to her eyes. 'Huh, and listen to this, Mama: "My dear boy is always caring and attentive". Dear boy indeed!' Ellen mocked. 'What about her estranged, dear friend?' She raged, and then a hand flew suddenly up to her mouth, and she gasped. 'Dear God, no… and now Anne's dog, Flossy, is dead! Poor Charlotte. It'll be like Anne dying all over again. Oh, Mama, I wish I was there with her.'

'Poor Charlotte,' Mrs Nussey said. 'But it's only a dog—'

'Yes, Anne's dog!' Ellen stressed. 'Charlotte's loving sister's dog. It'll bring it all back to her… oh, Mama, how can Charlotte ever recover when she is surrounded by so much sadness? By so much tyranny!'

Chapter Forty-One

Over the ensuing days and weeks the unstoppable flow of suffering continued and worsened. Tabby, troubled not only by illness, but succumbing to the disorders of an ageing body, after completing only a little dusting one morning, slumped into a chair in a corner of the dining room, panting and wheezing. Charlotte, sitting close by the fire, looked to her.

'Poor, Tabby!'

'Work... the thought of it fair wears me out,' she complained wearily. 'My old body is fit only for rest and sleep these days.'

She shuffled determinedly to the edge of her seat, clamped her hands around the chair arms and was about to haul herself up.

'Stay where you are, Tabby,' Charlotte ordered her.

'There's work to be done, and I, I'll...'

'Leave it, Tabby, Martha will do it tomorrow. She can bring her sister, Tabitha, to help out with the cleaning.'

'I've never shied away from a day's work in all my life.'

'Then it's time you took things easier. Work no more today, Tabby.'

'But I –'

'Go to your bed, Tabby, and sleep. Sleep for as long as you wish.'

The ageing servant, barely able to keep her eyes open, smiled and found within her the strength to chuckle.

'I've hardly the strength to rise from my chair.'

Tabby did rise from her chair. She made it to her bed, but never left it again unaided.

For as long as the servant clung on to life, Charlotte, though desperately ill herself, was determined to do all that she could in order to make life as comfortable as possible for their devoted ailing servant. She drew up a list of medicines and asked Martha to take it to the apothecary and procure what she could.

'Poor, dear, Tabby,' Mr Brontë said, hearing of the servant's plight from Martha when she returned from the apothecary, loaded with an armful of medicines. 'She's been with us an age, joining our family only a few years after we moved to Haworth... faithful servant and friend to the end. She's laughed with us, and she's cried with us. It'll indeed be a sad day God takes her,' he said, shaking his head, turning and shuffling disconsolately into his study.

Charlotte's decline continued and she grew progressively weaker. Sitting shivering by the fire one bitter March morning, she took a sheet of writing paper and picked up her pen...

"Dearest Nell,

The cold I caught last November has not properly left me and no amount of medicine seems able to bring about a cure. The doctor called yesterday – he calls almost daily – but is confident I will recover given time... I say this with qualification, Nell, but the doctor implied a happy event might not be far away, and has suggested that Arthur and me might like to think about preparing for busier days ahead! I remain cautious and worry but..."

Ellen tore open the envelope the instant Mercy put it into her hands and she quickly consumed its contents. Seconds later she gasped.

215

'Dear, God, no!'

'What is it, sister? What excites you so?'

'Charlotte... she, she's carrying a child, I'm sure.'

'And does Charlotte say she is?' Mrs Nussey asked, looking to Ellen, opening out her fan and fanning her face.

'She claims to have the symptoms: sickness of a morning and...'

'Charlotte will perhaps confirm it when she next visits,' Mrs Nussey said.

'If that wretched man she married ever allows her to visit again.'

The doctor called again and despite Charlotte's inability to respond to the medicines he prescribed, he remained positive still, insisting that there was no need for undue concern.

Worry, though, was an attribute that Mr Brontë could not easily brush aside and ignore. Charlotte was his last surviving child: his wife and five of his six children were already in their graves. Night after night he lay awake, troubled not only by Charlotte's illness, but also by the speed of Tabby's decline.

Arthur was traumatised and feared for his wife's life if she could not, or would not eat or drink anything. He attempted to tempt her with everything he could think of; the spoonful of water and wine he encouraged her to take had barely touched her tongue when she retched and spat it back out.

The doctor called yet again but by now, his abstracted stare and deep-furrowed brow suggested that he too, was becoming concerned. Baffled at Charlotte's inability to show even the slightest glimmer of improvement, he rummaged time and again through his medicine bag, reading and rereading every label on every bottle of medicine to see if he had a potion that might bring about a cure – a miracle tonic.

Nothing, it seemed, though, was capable of arresting Charlotte's decline. She no longer had the strength to stand and was unable to sit up in bed unsupported. The moans that had once troubled Mr Brontë were not now of pleasure, but of pain; pain from the body of his last surviving daughter, a daughter sinking a little more with each passing day. The resolve of everyone in the Brontë household, and beyond, was tested: it would be tested further over the coming days and weeks.

Chapter Forty-Two

Charlotte lay prostrate on her back in her bed, gaunt and pale, unable to eat or drink – unable to swallow the medicine that the doctor had prescribed. Her father, becoming increasingly desperate, carried a portion of bread and cheese into her room, but she baulked and turned nauseous at the sight of it.

'You'll not regain your strength, Charlotte, unless you take some nourishment,' he pleaded.

'Water, were I able to swallow it, comes straight back up,' she uttered and then a faint impression of a smile graced her cracked, dry lips. 'Tell me, Papa, how does Tabby do?'

'Worry not for Tabby, poor woman,' he said and sighed. 'She no longer lives in our home.'

'Papa… it was her abiding wish to spend her final hours in our home with us.'

'I know it was, but caring for two invalids is too much and I called on her nephew and asked him to remove her. He took her away yesterday.'

'Poor, Tabby.'

'She'll know nothing of it, Charlotte.'

Instead of the expected improvement the doctor felt would eventually come, Charlotte's decline continued. Thin and frail, her translucent skin was coloured only by the broad, dark circles that surrounded her eyes, eyes sunk almost from sight within seemingly deepening sockets.

Arthur was insensible with grief, wandering aimlessly from room to room. Emerging trance-like from the dining room, he looked about and then dashed into the kitchen. Finding Martha sitting on a stool sobbing, he halted abruptly, gesticulating awkwardly when she looked up to him through doleful, tearstained eyes.

'Mr Nicholls…' was all she could utter before more tears gushed and spilled from her eyes.

Arthur's lips moved, and it seemed that he would speak, offer comforting words to the distressed young servant. But he, too, was similarly anguished; overcome with grief and overwhelmed by the emotional turmoil that he suffered and he exited in the same agitated and distraught manner he had entered, without uttering a single word. He meandered about the hall, shuffling in one direction and then another, before charging upstairs. Stopping partway up, sniffing and mumbling, retracing his steps and then making a dash for Mr Brontë's study. He halted abruptly outside the door and formed a fist, but he turned and strode away and sought sanctuary in the dining room.

After pacing about, he settled in the chair by the fire – the chair that Charlotte sat when dreaming up her stories. And from her desk he took out a sheet of writing paper and picked up a pen – Charlotte's pen. He played with the pen between his fingers, raised it up to his lips and kissed it, before taking a deep breath and dipping the pen in the inkwell. With an unsteady hand wrote:

"Dear Ellen…"

Chapter Forty-Three

Ellen was restless and paced anxiously about the room. She was desperate for news from Charlotte and walked periodically to the window, looking out for the postman. The instant she saw him approaching she ran from the house to meet him, snatching the letters from his hand, smiling by way of apology for her rudeness, for her haste. Her smile, though, was crushed the instant her eyes fell upon the envelope: the address was written in a stranger's hand.

She hurried back inside, tearing open the envelope and snatching the letter from its sleeve, opening it out as she entered the living room.

'Dear, God, no!' Ellen shrieked, lowering herself onto the sofa, between her mother and Mercy. 'It's from him.'

'Him!'

'Nicholls!'

'And what does Mr Nicholls say?'

'"God makes us suffer terribly at this time, Charlotte especially. She remains gravely ill and shows not the slightest sign of improving.... To compound our misery, Tabby fell ill last week. The poor woman is now dead and buried..." Tabby, dead!' blurted Ellen. 'Poor Charlotte.'

'But what of Charlotte?' Mrs Nussey was impatient to know.

'She... she—' Ellen could speak no more.

'Go to her, Ellen,' Mrs Nussey implored. 'Charlotte is your dearest friend. You must neglect her no more.'

'How can I go to her, Mama?' Ellen said and sniffed. 'When that selfish man she married forbids it?' She drew an arm across her face and wiped away her tears.

'He'll deny you access to her no more,' Mrs Nussey said. 'Mercy, dear, help your sister pack her suitcase.'

Ellen's tears were replaced by anger.

'Nicholls, that wretched man has come between Charlotte and me since the day they were married – ever since they were courting. He wilfully obstructed our friendship. He was jealous, I'm sure. Charlotte should not have married him. Oh, Mama…'

Tears flowed, and Ellen sprang up off the sofa and began pacing about the room. Mercy went to her and took her into her arms. Mrs Nussey, sitting upright on the sofa, calmly opened out her fan and fanned her face. Her eyes, though, remained with her daughters and she waited until Ellen had regained a measure of composure, and then cleared her throat.

'You mustn't be too harsh on Mr Nicholls, Ellen, poor man. He suffers just as we do – more so.'

'Then why did he refuse me, Mama?' Ellen snapped. 'Why did he prevent me from going to Charlotte? Nicholls… his jealousy will send her to her grave.'

'Mr Nicholls did what he thought was best for Charlotte, even if it was ill advised,' Mrs Nussey said. 'He married Charlotte because he loves her.'

'Did Nicholls think I did not love her?' Ellen protested. 'Charlotte always got better when I was there to care for her.'

'Then do as Mama says, Ellen,' Mercy implored. 'Go to Charlotte, go and make her better. If Mr Nicholls truly loves her, he'll refuse you no more. And Charlotte will be desperate to see her friend. She'll be expecting you, praying for her nursemaid to come to her and make her better.'

'Mercy is right, Ellen,' their mother said. 'It's your duty as Charlotte's friend: do not forsake her when she needs you most.'

Arthur, clutching tight to a bonnet, wandered in and out of the hall, before dashing inside the dining room, re-emerging only seconds later, stopping at the foot of the stairs, looking up and listening. He stepped onto the stairs but retreated and shot into the kitchen. Martha looked to him; and through tearful eyes, watched as he lifted the bonnet he held in his hand up to his lips and kissed it.

'This was my wife's wedding bonnet, Martha,' he said, sniffing. 'Charlotte wore it– '

Martha sniffed. 'Did you want anything, Mr Nicholls?'

'Only for my wife to be well again,' he said, looking absently to her. But he shook his head. 'No, Martha, thank you... there is nothing.' He lowered himself onto a stool, sniffing and gesticulating. 'It's only a few months since Charlotte and me were married,' he said, stroking the bonnet that now rested on his lap. 'Charlotte wore this bonnet... she looked beautiful, like a little snowdrop – everybody said so. She was happy, and I the happiest man in all England. That happiness is slipping fast away, faster with each passing second.'

Chapter Forty-Four

Arthur, distant, despairing and tearful, lowered himself to his knees at Charlotte's bedside and rested his elbows on her bed. He clasped his hands tight together and bowed his head…

'Merciful Lord, please spare my wife, she—'

'Arthur…'

Charlotte's feint voice roused him. He lifted up his head and looked to her, leaned over and gathered her tenderly into his arms, pressing his cheek gently against hers.

'Darling, Charlotte… so cold—'

'God will not separate us, will he, Arthur, not now we are happy?'

'No, darling wife, no… he must not. I pray day and night he will not,' he said, kissing her cheek, her forehead, before laying her head back gently upon her pillow. 'The Lord cannot if he is truly merciful…'

For all his dedicated care, his pleas and his prayers, Charlotte's life ebbed away: one minute she was there, and in the next she was gone.

'No, no…' blurted Arthur, taking her limp hand into his, lifting it up and pressing it against his lips, kissing her fingers. He then lowered her hand upon her breast, leaned over and kissed Charlotte's forehead, her cheek, and her lips and then rested his convulsing head upon his wife's stilled stomach.

Mr Brontë, alerted by his son-in-law's cries, by his sobbing, hauled himself up the stairs and shuffled toward their room. The door was ajar and he looked inside and saw Arthur, his head upon Charlotte's lifeless body, jerking to the rhythm of his sobbing.

'May the Lord have mercy on my poor daughter's soul – upon us all,' Mr Brontë uttered, as he traced the sign of a cross across his breast. 'Amen.'

'Mr Brontë, she…' Arthur blurted, turning and looking to him through tearful and bloodshot eyes.

Mr Brontë nodded; he bowed his head, and then turned and walked solemnly away.

Martha, tearful and distraught, meandered about the kitchen; she stepped into the hall and saw Mr Brontë's study door wide open. She looked inside, retreated and looked next in the dining room. Seeing it empty she trundled slowly toward the stairs, halting upon hearing noises up above. And she stood there, shuffling unsteadily, looking up and listening for some minutes to the unsettling sound of men sobbing. She then climbed up the stairs and stepped tentatively toward Mr Brontë's room. The door was ajar. Martha angled her head close to it and listened…

'Why, Lord, why take Charlotte… my last surviving child? She—'

Martha cleared her throat and then knocked on the door.

'Mr Brontë.'

'Martha… come,' he said.

She opened the door and stepped cautiously inside, looking on as Mr Brontë struggled to his feet. He turned and faced her.

'I'm ever so sorry, Mr Brontë, but I, I…' The young servant, overcome with grief, could speak no more.

Mr Brontë reached out and placed a comforting hand

upon her shoulder, and then pulled a handkerchief out from a pocket; he shook it open and handed it to her. Martha took it from him; she dried her tears and blew her nose noisily, and then offered the handkerchief back.

'Keep it, Martha,' Mr Brontë said. 'I have no use of it anymore… I have no tears left to dry,' he said and paused, staring abstractedly at her. 'All are now gone now, Martha… Charlotte has gone home: she has gone to be with her sisters, her brother and her mother.'

'Oh, Mr Brontë…' Martha blurted, dabbing the tears that spilled from her eyes. 'But why Charlotte?'

'The ways of the Lord, Martha,' he said and sighed. 'Cruel and mysterious, but there it is. What can we mere mortals do?'

Mr Brontë's resolve lasted only seconds more before his lips began to quiver and he stumbled forward into Martha's opening arms.

'Oh, Mr Brontë!' she cried out, catching him.

'My wife, my six children are all gone, gone to their graves before me… God, it seems, sees fit that I should suffer alone on this earth. What, I ask, were my sins, Martha?'

The young servant looked askance to him; she shook her head but said nothing. They both remained speechless for some minutes, and the only sound was of their sobbing.

Chapter Forty-Five

The next morning a carriage sped along the lane and drew to a halt outside the parsonage. The coachman jumped down, opened the door and Ellen hurried out. She ran ungainly along the garden path, knocked on the parsonage door, opened it and entered.

Martha flew out from the kitchen, stopping abruptly only inches from Ellen, and then burst into tears. Ellen, rigid and horrified, stared at the servant for some seconds, before gathering the weeping girl into her arms.

'I dared not think it before, but now I know I am come too late.'

'Oh, Miss Nussey.' Martha cried. 'If only you'd come sooner: Charlotte always got better when you were here to care for her.'

'That I had been granted permission,' Ellen said softly.

They remained locked together in each other's arms for some minutes, sobbing and then Ellen let go of Martha. Sniffing, she braced herself, inhaling and exhaling deeply as she attempted to stem her tears. She untied the ribbons on her bonnet and looked about. 'And Mr Brontë… where is the poor man, Martha?'

Martha nodded in the direction of his study. Ellen took off her coat and bonnet and hung them on the coat stand and then, after composing herself, she turned to the still-sobbing servant.

'No more tears, now, Martha! We must both be strong for Mr Brontë's sake,' she said, and then strode toward his study. She knocked on the door, opened it and stepped inside.

Mr Brontë, sitting at his desk, holding the magnifying glass over a page of the bible, turned. In his haste to stand, the glass slipped from his fingers and fell onto his desk.

'Ellen.' he cried out, shuffling unsteadily and stumbling into her opening arms.

'I'm sorry, Mr Brontë... I, I came as quickly as I could. It was not soon enough,' she said, and then burst into tears. 'Poor, poor Charlotte, she...'

Ellen could speak no more and she and Mr Brontë remained locked in each other's embrace, until the bereft parson calmed himself. He lowered Ellen down onto his chair, pulled up a stool and sat opposite and then took Ellen's hands into his. Through moist and bloodshot eyes, he looked directly into hers.

'I knew it all along, Ellen... knew my daughter's constitution was not strong enough to withstand marriage. That's why I, I... Oh, Ellen...' Tears stopped his words and Ellen withdrew her hands from his. She leaned forward and drew his head onto her breast and held it there.

*

Arthur stood alone in the churchyard, watching the mourners shuffling solemnly away. Some meandered in the direction of the parsonage, where refreshments had been prepared; ale and wine to slake their thirsts, food to settle empty and grumbling stomachs; others walked away to grieve in the privacy of their homes. Arthur took a handkerchief from a pocket, dabbed his eyes and blew his nose, but then he saw Ellen approaching and quickly pushed it back inside his pocket.

Through her pain and sadness, Ellen summoned the strength to smile.

'Mr Nicholls… I know, from what Charlotte told me, that she loved you dearly. You brought joy back into her life after the years of sadness… you enriched her final months more than anyone else could. Charlotte loved you, Mr Nicholls, really and truly—'

'My dear, Ellen…' he cut in. 'Charlotte loved you also. More, perhaps, than she loved me. You were the one true friend she cherished above all others; she trusted in you absolutely,' he said, gesticulating awkwardly. 'I, I did what I thought was right and best, Ellen, bestowing the love and care expected of a husband. But I should have sent for you. I should have sent for you when Charlotte first fell ill. I was selfish and wanted to care for her myself, but…' Sniffing, he faltered and halted, but he inhaled and then continued. 'In, in doing so I fear I made you and Charlotte strangers. For that, Ellen, I am truly sorry,' he said and sniffed. 'I hope… hope you'll…'

'Well…' Ellen interjected. 'Let's not make strangers of each other, Mr Nicholls.'

'No, Ellen, no… we must not – will not,' he said earnestly, but then in his next breath as Ellen readied herself to move away, he gesticulated uncomfortably, and in a nervy, stuttering voice, added. 'You, you will maintain your promise, won't you, Ellen…?'

'Promise…?'

'And destroy all correspondence pertaining to Charlotte – burn every last trace of it.'

That he should speak of such a contentious issue, and on such a solemn occasion incensed Ellen. Outwardly she did not show it for reasons of propriety, nor did she wish to mouth to him another blatant lie. Holding him in a stern stare for some seconds, she nodded, but only with fierce reluctance; and then she turned from him and strode away. Rage contorted Ellen's soft and gentle features in a way that was alien to her to her nature.

Life, or some semblance of life, returned to the parsonage. Resurrected temporarily by the presence of the mourners gathered in celebration of the life that had passed, the life of Charlotte Brontë. There were people present who were her friends; and there were those that knew of her only through her novels; others knew her as the daughter of the parson of Haworth; and there were people present that hardly knew her at all, but all were equally welcome.

Martha's eyes were dry for the first time in days. Being in charge of refreshments, she was preoccupied – too busy for emotional indulgences. Much of the morning, she and her sister, Tabitha, had been busy preparing food – a feast that her former colleague, Tabby, would have approved of. Tabitha cut and buttered the bread, carved the joints of meat and made the sandwiches, while Martha dashed about organising everything, carrying plates of food into the dining room – a task that continued for as long as there were hungry mouths to feed, or until supplies had all been exhausted.

Mr Brontë, his spirits having sufficiently recovered, circulated among the mourners and, despite his own appalling loss and his sadness, he summoned within his crushed constitution the strength to offer a consoling word, a comforting hand, or a prayer to anyone needier than he – if such a person existed.

Chapter Forty-Six

When the mourners had all departed and gone away to their homes, Mr Brontë stood alone on the steps outside the parsonage, looking out over the garden. Recalling perhaps happier times, to the day long ago when, with his wife Maria and their six children, they arrived in Haworth and settled into the hilltop parsonage. If he closed his eyes he could see their smiling faces still, vivid and alive; bright faces of lively, intelligent and talented children, but they were gone now, taken from him much too soon. Never would he again touch their flesh, hear their voices or see those familiar happy faces, and the pain would torture and torment him until the world was lost to him. Without his faith, life would be utterly desolate, without purpose and without hope for memories alone, though they provide comfort, can never be enough.

A warm and gentle breeze teased his senses and he turned his head into its balm and listened for the voices of his children. When they failed to sing, he shuffled inside his soulless home and closed the door.

He wandered into the dining room, smiling involuntarily on seeing his son-in-law, lost to his own sad thoughts, sitting by the fire. Arthur, though, had not yet seen him: his empty stare was trained upon the grey smoke rising up from the burning coals and disappearing up the chimney – like life, vanishing before his eyes.

Both men looked simultaneously to the empty chair by

the fire, the chair that Charlotte sat when dreaming up her stories. Arthur looked next to Mr Brontë and acknowledged his presence with a nod, with an empty smile and then he watched as his father-in-law shuffled nearer and sat in the chair opposite, in Charlotte's chair.

The bereaved men sat a moment in silence, listening to the clock's relentless and restless tick, counting down their seconds, their minutes, and their hours. Then Mr Brontë cleared his throat.

'You'll take off now, I expect, Arthur? Seek out more profitable pastures?'

'No, Mr Brontë,' he replied, askance and furrowing his brow. 'Charlotte and I made a vow. One that I will not renege on.'

'A vow!'

'Before we were married, Charlotte made me promise that, should anything happen to her, I would remain at the parsonage with you for as long as you live. I will honour that promise, Mr Brontë. I will keep it if you live to be a hundred. If it is your wish also.'

Mr Brontë nodded and he forced a smile.

'Then I can put my pistol away.'

'Put your pistol away, Mr Brontë!' Mr Nicholls repeated.

'The need for it has passed. I have no children to protect anymore,' he said, staring distractedly and sighing. 'A lifetime's servitude to God had failed me. God has failed me… taken all and left me alone on this earth with nothing, with no one—'

'But I am here still. We have yet each other, Mr Brontë. The good Lord has left you and me behind for a purpose, to spread to the world the word of a dear daughter and wife – of the celebrated novelist, Charlotte Brontë.'

'Charlotte Nicholls!' Mr Brontë corrected him.

'Charlotte Brontë is the name on her books. Charlotte Brontë is the name she is known to everyone throughout England – throughout the world. Charlotte Brontë will not die. She will live eternally in the hearts of her readers – as I'm sure will Emily and Anne – for as long as earth exists. Long after Arthur Bell Nicholls, Charlotte's devoted and heartbroken husband, has withered away and has long been forgotten.'

Over the coming months and years, Mr Brontë and Mr Nicholls shared many solemn days and lonely nights, preserving and treasuring in their hearts fond memories of a dear daughter and wife: memories that would never fade, memories that, whenever their spirits faltered, gave them the strength to carry on.

Mr Brontë carried those memories in his injured heart until the day that he, too, was reunited with his wife and their six children. Mr Nicholls kept his promise to Charlotte, living and working at the parsonage in Haworth. Serving his father-in-law for the six further years that Mr Brontë lived.

Reverend Patrick Brontë died on 7th June 1861; and Mr Nicholls returned to Ireland. Arthur Nicholls' love for Charlotte never waned, dying only with his last breath on 2nd December 1906.

Source Material

Although *Mutable Passions* is a work of fiction, it is based on fact and the following are the principal books used.

Barker, Juliet, *The Brontës* (1995, London), Phoenix, Orion
—— *The Brontës: A Life in Letters* (1997, Harmondsworth), Viking, Penguin

Brontë, Charlotte, *Jane Eyre* (1996, London), Penguin Classics
—— *Villette* (2000 Oxford), OUP

Gaskell, Elizabeth, *The Life of Charlotte Brontë* (1997, Manchester), Penguin Classics

Gérin, Winifred, *Charlotte Brontë* (1967, Oxford), OUP
—— *Emily Brontë* (1979, Oxford), OUP
——*Anne Brontë* (1976, London), Allen Lane, Penguin Books

Leyland, Francis, *The Brontë Family* (1973, Manchester), EJ Morten

Lock, John & Canon WT Dixon, *A Man of Sorrow* (1965, London), Thomas Nelson

Shorter, Clement, *The Brontës and their Circle* (1896, London), JM Dent & Sons